THE TREE OF
THE FOLKUNGS

I: FOLKE FILBYTER

THE
TREE OF THE
FOLKUNGS

I: FOLKE FILBYTER

VERNER VON HEIDENSTAM

GYLDENDAL

10 & 12 Orange Street, London, W. C. 2
and Copenhagen
1925

CONTENTS

TRANSLATOR'S NOTE

A few indications may be useful in giving the reader the main historical bearings of this romance. For the early history of Sweden we are dependent on Sagas, the historical character of which decreases with the distance of time separating the events recorded from the writing of the record, though the Sagas are usually based on older material, often in poetic form. The names of the Kings, at any rate, may be taken as authentic, but even in the 11th century some uncertainty lingers as to dates.

Some time in the 8th century there reigned at Upsala a powerful King named Ivar Vidfadme (Wide-embrace), who is said in the Saga to have conquered a fifth part of England, and from whom all subsequent Swedish Kings claimed descent, down to the year 1060. The next King we need note is Erik the Victorious, who shared the kingdom with his brother Olaf. After Olaf's death, his son, Styrbjörn the Strong, claimed a share in the government, but was defeated and slain by Erik at the battle of Fyrisvall, near Upsala, in 983. Erik died about ten years later and was succeeded by his son Olaf Skottkonung (Tax-King), who took part in the alliance against Olaf Tryggvason of Norway and was present, with little honour, at the naval battle of Svolder. Emund the Old, a son of Olaf Skottkonung, died in 1060, the last of the old line of kings.

It is here that our story begins, at the close of the Viking Age, a period which was marked, in Sweden, by a prolonged struggle between Christianity and heathenism, by civil war among rival claimants to the throne, and by general insecurity. There was as yet no nobility; power was in the hands of the free owners of the soil and they exercised it at their assemblies or Things. The sources of wealth were two: the land, and plunder taken abroad on viking raids. From obscure origins in these conditions came the powerful family of the Folkungs, which was destined later to bring Sweden into line with the

other kingdoms of mediæval Europe. Paganism died hard at
Upsala; the First Part of this book ends with its final sup-
pression by King Inge.

The two centuries which elapse between the First and Second
Parts were filled with wars of succession, the country generally
remaining in a backward state. In the time of King Sverker
—grandson of Blot Sven, the last heathen King—the Swedes
and Goths became united. Erik IX (Erik I in the new reckon-
ing) did much to advance the Church in Sweden and carried
on crusades in heathen Finland. After his death in 1160 he
was long venerated by the Swedes as Saint Erik, although he
was never canonized. Meanwhile the tree of the Folkungs was
growing and the family became dominant early in the 13th
century, gradually making its way towards the throne. Birger,
the most powerful member of this clan and one of the builders
of Sweden, became in 1247 Earl to his brother-in-law, King
Erik III, and suppressed the revolt of Holmger, son of the last
King, Knut the Tall. Holmger was executed in 1248 and
buried in the convent of Sko.

Here the curtain rises on the Second Part of our story, when
Earl Birger is the real ruler of Sweden, having set his little
son Valdemar on the throne. Further elucidation is unneces-
sary, but one or two dates may be of interest. The battle of
Hofva, described in Chapter XVII, was fought in June, 1275,
and Magnus (surnamed Ladulås, i.e., Barnlock) was elected
King a few months later. Magnus died at Vising Isle in 1290,
his deposed brother Valdemar outliving him thirteen years.
The family rapidly died out. The last of the Folkungs to be
mentioned in history was Magnus Eriksson (grandson of
Magnus Ladulås), who inherited the throne of Norway from
his maternal grandfather, Haakon V, and at the same time (at
the age of three) became King of Sweden. (This is the young
King Magnus who is introduced in Sigrid Undset's historical
novel, *The Mistress of Husaby*.) Both kingdoms were taken
from him before he died.

Such explanatory notes as seemed necessary have been placed
at the end of the book and are referred to by numbers in the
text.

PART I
FOLKE FILBYTER

I

How the dwarfs lost the horn Månegarm and how a seed was laid in the earth from which a great tree was to grow, is here to be related. Here we shall tell the story of a race which attained to the highest honour and then was swept away and left no trace behind. What thoughts the mighty ones of this kin had of their golden crowns, when their old age lay before them like cold and slippery stairs descending to hell, and how the unhappy ones lamented their fetters, shall also be told. Let those who will hear these things give heed. Nothing shall be kept back. Vast distances separate them from us, but all human destinies are spun by the same weird sisters.

On the east coast of Sweden lies a deep and rocky bay. A shield maiden had there been buried in her chair, in full armour, with spear on shoulder. Her mound was the highest in the district and was seen from afar as a beacon for seafarers.

Many memorial stones were set up along the shore, some mossy and unhewn, others carved with runes. No road led thither and it was far to any town or homestead. In wintertime the tracks of men were seldom to be seen, though there was room for thirty ships to lie drawn up in the snow, well roofed over with birch-bark and branches of spruce. The vikings did not come down to the coast till after the month of Goi, when spring was approaching.[1] They brought tools and timber with them in their sledges and were accompanied by a number of traders, who pitched their tents of frieze in a circle around the shield maiden's mound. Then for some weeks the place was as full of life as a Thing-stead; axes rang and tar-cauldrons bubbled till the ships were launched and put to sea. After that the district lay as desolate as before.

One day in late autumn a heavy gale was blowing from seaward. The gulls were flung back by the blast and settled like

[1] The old Scandinavian month of Goi began about the middle of February.

3

crows upon the fields inland. A wall of cloud stood over the sea, so that the sun went down without the glow of evening. In a rift of a storm-cloud which lay above the burial-place the first constellation was already sparkling.

That evening a Finn dwarf, Jorgrimme by name, stood upon the shield maiden's mound. He was clad entirely in rough fox-skins. His magic drum hung on his back, and in the silver chain which served him as a belt he carried a number of thunderbolts and stone knives. He stood with his back to the sea, looking inland. At last he raised both thumbs and bent down, calling into the mound:

"Mound-dwellers! Do you hear? This night the women weep in the hall of Fyrisvall. Long is the way thither, seven days' journey, but never before did I hear such wailing. Never before did such terror fare over the land."

He searched for a while in the frozen grass and collected some dry herbs; then he stopped again, listening.

"Strike thy shield hard, mound-maiden!" he said. "Rouse thy peers from the sleep of death! Now creak the floor-planks behind the stone of sacrifice in the Sveas' holiest temple. It is Asa Thor's image that is trembling. Mercy, mercy upon all that has life!"

While he was yet speaking, a fleet of homeward-bound vikings appeared on the horizon. All the ships came on in line abreast with straining masts and swelling sails. The bellowing note of a lur sounded through the storm, and at the signal three of the ships fell off the wind and made for the shield maiden's mound.

The others tore onward to the east in a cloud of driving snow and rounded the point of land to the north. They were the ships of the grave and warlike Upland Sveas, two and twenty in number. And threatening they looked with the death runes on their sails and their figure-heads of gaping dragons, grinning boars and charging bulls wrestling with the wintry Baltic. They had to reach the inland waters of Sigtuna before the ice stopped them, and some were bound as far as the reedy marshes of Aros. There the smoke of fat offerings would greet them from every rock. The priestesses would come down to the water's edge and bless the ships, sprinkling them with blood and waving branches of the evergreen-tree, the sacred tree that grew by the mound of

Upsala. For all this the Sveas were longing and would take no reef in their sails. They had sworn an oath never to avoid a squall or run for shelter.

The central ship of the three which had bidden the others farewell with the notes of the lur, bore Freya's head on her stem. But it had grown so big at last with all the icicles hanging or sprouting from it that nothing could be distinguished of the frank and fair features of Vanadis in this ever-growing sea-monster.[2] Wherefore the captain of the stem, who sat fully armed in the fore part of the ship, took his ax and broke off the ice, and then unshipped the head, laying it under the thwarts, lest it might scare the spirits of the land. The ship was called by the goddess' byname Menglöd, which was painted in great runes across the sail. Yet there was no sign of Freya's joyful spirit on board, though the crew was made up of golden-haired folk who dwelt south of the forests and who might spend the winter in riding from feast to feast to dance and play.[3] To mark their return, all the shields were set up along the gunwale, but there was grumbling and dissension on board. Every time the prow-man bent down to point the course, he threw abusive language aft. Even the helmsman, who laid his whole weight upon the steering-oar without taking his eyes from the grave-mound beneath the storm-cloud, spoke so loudly of his discontent that none needed to ask his thoughts. For this was a custom among the Goths of that coast: so long as they were on war service or out a-viking they obeyed their leader blindly and without a word, but the time that elapsed between sighting their home country and dropping anchor they might freely employ in showering upon him all the blame and scorn that had gathered in their minds during the voyage. It was open to them to praise him in a heroic ballad or to compare him with the most contemptible things they could think of. And this was just what they made haste to do with all their hearts. They cried that never had oak planks been dishonoured by supporting a fatter pig more ready for the slaughter. Only one man

[2] Vanadis and Menglöd (necklace-glad) were among the names of the goddess Freya.

[3] South of the great forests of Kolmorden and Tiveden is Götaland, the land of the Goths; north of the forests is Sveland, the land of the Swedes. This primary distinction is of great importance in the early history of the country.

kept obstinately silent: he was the butt of their ridicule, who lately had commanded them all, Folke Filbyter, the chief, the sea-king.

He sat in the stern, farthest aft, half a man's height above the helmsman and a whole man's height above the rest of the crew. His helmet bore as a crest the upturned wing of a sea-eagle, which made him still taller, and yet he seemed not quite the man for so honourable a place. The gale had plucked his crest of half its feathers and his cloak was full of patches, with long and crooked stitches which showed that he had put them in himself. His shoulders were broad and rounded, and his bony arms, perfectly bare, seemed to possess the wiry strength of one who digs and carries. His flaxen hair, white in the dusk, was caught by the wind and wound about his chin and cheeks, giving him a womanly aspect strangely at variance with his big and heavy limbs. But whenever his hair was blown from his face, it disclosed the glum and furrowed features of a peasant.

He looked out over the skerries, where the seals jostled each other for a good sleeping-place or stood upright in the surf searching for an ice-floe to carry them to sea for the winter. When he heard their weird barking and scolding, he shook with huge merriment. This was the only sign that his hearing was alert although he sat in silence.

The man at the bows was now lying almost prone over the stem on the look-out for shoals, and he was a wild, scarred berserk. He put his hand behind his back, and its palm came down on the head of a little old man, who sat with his legs crossed around the mast.

"Speak, thrall!" said the prow-man. "We took you with us to cook our victuals and to guard the water-vat, and well have you done your duty. Not more than twice or thrice have you been flogged. But we have not yet heard what you think of the chief. Speak out now, thrall. If you can liken him to anything better than a sow, you have a nimbler tongue than I."

The thrall began at once obediently to mimic a ship's skald by plucking the stay with his fingers like a harp-string. His red-veined nose had the soft, fine curve of all the cheerful Gothland folk, and he made his mouth small and merry like that of a goat-girl eating whortleberries. Singing through his nose, he turned to the crew and began:

"Fair was the bark as she mirrored her Freya's head in Niörva Sound.[4] We saw the mountains of Blåland, but naught did our chief see.[5] He saw not the women at play, when they went out into the water to bathe. Without striking a blow we might have taken them with us. Nor did he ever challenge famous champions to single combat. And in the churches, when we spat in the face of Christ's Mother, he thrust us aside to pluck the gold ring from her finger. All he strove for was gold and silver. Not much did we know of him when first he shipped us, for he came from distant parts. But in every dispute he would boast of his lineage. A peasant was his father and a peasant his grandfather, and a peasant's bickering will never leave him. It will descend to his children, if he ever has any. But I scarce think he is man enough for that."

"We have a more skilful skald on board than any of us had thought," said the prow-man.

The thrall grew bolder yet and sang:

"Then the wind drove us to the unfriendly coasts of Jorsalaland.[6] There at last our chief's eyes grew wide. There he went ashore and stared about him till evening. What he saw was that the mills were driven by the wind, so that the millers had only to hold out their sacks and get them filled. Never had he heard of so great a marvel. He talked of nothing else for the rest of the voyage, when we all wanted to sleep. Chief, have you understood my words? Now we are at home! Meal-king, go now and hoist your meal-sail!"

"I shall!" answered Folke Filbyter, standing up. Now at last it was his right to reply. "Are you not all from the land of meal-dust, south of the forests? If it were summer, I should fancy even here I heard the murmur of the cornfields of the golden East. Truly, prow-man, yon old man by the mast has a quicker tongue than you."

The men fell silent with suppressed mutterings, and two of them stepped into the water and carried Folke Filbyter ashore. With a broad, sure tread he ascended the mound, without paying much heed to the dwarf, who was still standing there

---

[4] Niörva Sound is the Straits of Gibraltar.

[5] Blåland is the North of Africa: the country of "blue" or black men.

[6] Jorsalaland is the Holy Land (Jorsala-Jerusalem).

with his face turned inland. From the pouch of his ragged cloak the chief took out a handful of earth and threw it upon the grass. Then he bent forward and addressed the shield maiden in the stone chamber below, as was the wont of returned vikings.

"When I set out," he said, "I took this mould from your mound that it might bring me luck. Generously have you helped me. Poor was I when I sailed, driven from my father's house, where too many sons thronged the bench. Homeless I was as the wailing guillemot under the autumn sky. Since then I have never drained a horn under sooty roof-tree, nor slept in downy bed, but seven strongholds have I burnt in Frankland. Now I am rich enough to buy land for myself, and I am sick and weary of the sea, which my murmuring crew are so unwilling to leave. The servants of the sea are thralls of a fickle master. Thralls, too, are they who writhe in longing for fame or who see in all their dreams a woman. Therefore my men are thralls, but I alone am free, for I have no longing and I love no woman nor anything under the sun. Mound-woman, when did so free a man speak with you? When did so happy a man stand upon your grave? Here I offer to you my tokens of thraldom, my helmet and my sword. The world may go as it will for me. I shall enjoy my years in peace. Early each morning I shall go to my trap to fetch what it has caught that night. Then I shall doze upon my seat of turf in the sunshine and hear the corn growing."

He thrust his sword deep into the grass and hung his chief's helm upon the hilt, so that he stood bare-headed.

"And I tell you that you would do better to go back to your ship," answered the dwarf, with a shrill cry. "I tell you, chief, I tell you, franklin, that if it is peace you seek, you must fly. For generations without number no man has beheld such things as are now at hand. The Æsir are now descending upon the land to seek out a seed of vigorous growth, and no man knows where their choice may fall. They will not choose the fairest or the noblest, but that which promises the strongest shoot. From this seed will grow a shady tree with tempests and calm stars in its topmost branches. So high shall the tree rise that it will overshadow all living things, not only men but the steeds in their stalls and the oxen at the plough, nay, even the wild beasts in the woods. For when its boughs drip sunshine or blood, all will feel it. And all will be hurt when the stem is rent and falls. Thus do the high Æsir speak by me to-night."

Folke Filbyter advanced towards the dwarf and shook his fist above his cap.

"Practise your sorcery upon the dead beneath their mounds, dwarf, and let the living take care of themselves! I believe in no gods, but in my own strength. It is a far cry to the mighty ones at Fyrisvall, and in their field I have no mind to dig. And now, my men, bring hither the sack and the dice and the balance, and let us divide the booty before it grows darker. The Great Wain and Freya's Spinning-wheel are already kindled in the sky."

The bay glittered in the last rays of evening like a network of innumerable wet meshes, and the men stood up to their knees in the water as they brought the cargo ashore. They could not hear him for the rumbling of the storm, but understood his gestures. On other voyages their ships had been filled to the gunwale with arms, bales of cloth, wine-skins and bags of walnuts and spices. This time there was nothing but a single sack, but it held gold and silver in coin or melted down. It took many men to get it up to the mound.

Folke Filbyter broke the seals and plunged his hand into the coins and gold bars, as a farmer sifts the seed through his fingers to see if it is good. Then with scrupulous care he weighed out to every man his promised share. Thus the men were bound to stay and see the ships beached and shored up. Last of all, lots were cast in the prow-man's helmet for the Norns' gift. Every man who threw at least five might take as much as would lie in his open hand. But when the outstretched hands had been filled, the miserly Folke Filbyter swept back into the sack as many coins as he could reach in haste.

"A good chief claims tribute as his due," he said, and quickly tied up the sack again.

With great difficulty he hoisted it on to his back. He looked like a beggar with his scrip as he walked away over the burial-place. The sack was so heavy that he often had to stop and lean against the standing stones.

"Mound-dwellers!" cried the dwarf, turning again to landward. "I hear the brides of the sacrifice opening the gates of Upsala temple, and in the court of the king's house servants are running with tapers. I see a white-bearded old man lying in his closed bed with open and motionless eyes. Now dies the last king of Ivar Vidfadme's race."

II

OR two nights Folke Filbyter wandered through the woods, where a thin coat of snow already lay upon the ground. In the day-time he hid under bushes and branches for fear of robbers, and even in his sleep he clasped the sack.

When the third day was half done, he threw himself down on a low hillock in the forest. It was so thickly overgrown with young spruce that no snow had reached it. Only in one place the tree-tops were thin enough to give him a view of the sun's whole disk, but it was beginning to sink and spin and change colour. His head involuntarily dropped to one side, so that his ear came on the ground. He had nothing to eat or drink, and the snow that he laid on his tongue from time to time burned more than it refreshed him. He fought against sleep by forcing his ears to listen and his eyes to look at the reeling sun.

"I had fallen asleep," he said, sitting up. His eyes had really closed and he had been asleep, though no longer than a breath or two. But his hearing, which alone remained awake, was thus made doubly keen. He was sure that the ground under his ear shook with a peculiar sound. When he had once begun to listen, he could hear it even when he sat upright. It sounded something like a dance, but there was no stamping of shoes or smacking of bare feet; the steps were soft and muffled. Someone was beating time on a drum-skin, but only with his nails, for it sounded like a bird hopping on a birch-bark roof. A sour smell of smoke stung his nose, and as he had not yet opened his eyes it was as though he had fallen asleep in earnest and was dreaming of clearings and the dwellings of friendly men. But then he remembered his sack, and, grasping it anew, he looked up.

He crept cautiously forward to try whether the sound was louder and nearer at any spot. When he had gone half-way round the knoll, he found that the smoke grew thicker and that was what distorted the sun and made it quiver. He felt his way another arm's length through the brushwood and then, instead of the prickly pine-needles under his fingers, he felt something smooth and soft, as though he had been stroking a dog's back. It was a curtain of skin. It slipped aside at his touch, disclosing a narrow entrance that led into the lighted interior of the mound. It was so full of smoke that at first he could distinguish nothing but a few crackling sticks under a pot and some legs in shaggy socks dancing round the earthen floor. By degrees he discovered in the far corner, above some hunting-gear and gnawed bones, a pair of hands drumming with their nails on a skin. The people of the mound whispered continually in time with the drum, always taking care that each word was spoken as though by one voice. They repeated again and again the same invocation: "Stone Eye, Stone Brow, God of the Fosse, Umasumbla, help us!"

He drew the skin back across the entrance and grasped his sack again, fully determined to stay no longer than he could help among such mysterious beings. But scarcely had he hoisted the burden on to his aching back when he heard a dwarf woman pant out the words, without losing the rhythm of the chant: "Father, father, I hear the baying of the moon-hound. Månegarm's gaping jaws are ready to swallow the pale winter sun. Father, father, fill me the horn, for now I faint!"

A lid of clay was raised from a pitcher and there was a sound of splashing and bubbling as the drink ran into the horn. Then he could no longer control his thirst and violently flung the skin aside. The smoke at once rushed out and he saw two dwarf girls holding each other by the hand and circling round continually on the same spot. On seeing him, they dropped each other's hands and tottered backward to the walls, their wild eyes shining like bubbles of blood. They were entirely naked, with very slender arms and legs and little projecting breasts. They wore nothing on their yellow bodies but some dangling strings of glass beads, and on their feet they had soft socks of foxes' skin, which were not able to prevent the shaking of the floor. A dwarf man, who seemed well on in years, though his plaited hair was black as the raven's wing, rose startled from the heap of bones in the corner. He thrust aside his drum and smacked his tongue on the roof of his mouth and spoke with his thumbs after the manner of Finn folk.

"Wanderer by secret paths, worshipper of the Æsir," he said, his eyes filling with false tears, "you do very ill to steal upon the dwarf in his hole."

The smoke stuck in Folke Filbyter's dry throat and it was some time before he could answer; so the dwarf went on:

"Very ill have you done, for this place is not for unhallowed eyes. Know you not, stranger, that when we dwarfs dance we never stop until we fall? Then our heart leaps into our head, so that we feel it throbbing in our temples. And then we lie giddy on the ground, communing with the One-eyed, the God of the Fosse, the cruel and bloodthirsty one who has power over us. He tells us all that is happening and is to happen. And much did he tell us this morning. But what seek you here? Will you buy smith's work of the dwarf, or thunderbolts?"

"I have come into a tract of cairns and caves!" Folke Filbyter hurled the words into the mound as soon as he could speak again. "If this is a holy place, it will not be profaned by a good deed. A hungry and thirsty man, shaking with cold, asks but a quickening draught from the horn. Come out, old man, instead of plucking your hair and moaning. Judge for yourself whether an unarmed man with a sack on his back has any look of evil purpose."

"Even on cairns and caves there grows fresh grass each summer," replied the dwarf. "But what is now to grow we must inquire of the One-eyed with our dancing. My daughters, shall we ask him, too, what this wanderer carries in his sack?"

Folke Filbyter gave a start and shifted a little to one side.

"My sack holds shreds and patches and old shoes, and a bare-headed unarmed man is safest from peace-breakers. Tell me now, is it far to the haunts of men?"

"Strange shreds and patches from their rattling," said the dwarf with flashing eyes, but without appearing to notice his uneasiness. "Drops of other men's sweat you have in your sack, but they have turned so hard that they ring against one another. Plunder is a heavy burden and you have a long way to the haunts of men. Where men build homes and set up landmarks, the dwarf must needs depart. The dwarf remembers neither father nor mother, knows not whence he came. Lonely he lives in the woods with his daughters. Every omen strikes fear into him, and all the autumn threatening constellations have appeared in the sky. A good king has long reigned over the land. Fair was his greeting as he rode to the Thing in the white crown of his age. Far into the woods was heard the clashing of shields and the shouting of the free udalmen as they announced their will to him. Emund was of ancient lineage, descended from the gods, and he oppressed no man. The smoke rose calmly from the dwarf's cave, and those who sacrificed to Thor and Frey had his protection. Therefore the Christian folk called him the Bad, but we others called him the Old. Of a surety is he now dead, and I tell you, wanderer, that he has left no son."

"You dwarfs think you know everything," answered Folke Filbyter. "And now I see that it was you who stood upon the shield maiden's mound. Had you shown me the shortest path, you would have saved me much wandering. But what does it concern me who is master of the fortunes of Upsala? A king is a drone, who plays the master at a feast where others bear the cost. My fathers were stout-hearted udalmen and none of them ever sold himself for the king's pay. Give me the horn now, manikin!"

The dwarf hissed scornfully through his front teeth and pressed both thumbs against his chest.

"Have you never heard of the greatest treasure of Jorgrimme's hole? Have you never heard of the wolfhound Månegarm who pursues the moon with howls and barking to swallow it up? A craftsman of old once took a bull's horn and set it upon feet and sang runes over it. He washed it in sweet hemlock, which makes men mad, and in witches' herbs to make them stiff and hard. This horn he named after the wolfhound, for he who drinks from it is seized with a feeling of such wild triumph that he would swallow the moon and the stars and all that is to be seen. At last the craftsman took fright at his own work and hid it in the hollow trunk of a tree high up on a mountain. The bees built their combs about the horn and filled them with honey, but Jorgrimme took counsel of his gods and found the treasure. Is it from the horn Månegarm you would quench your thirst? It is much to ask."

"I no more believe in your wolfhounds than in your gods."

Jorgrimme slowly approached the entrance with the pitcher in one hand and the dripping horn in the other. It was a short, stumpy bull's horn on two clumsy iron feet with a rude iron ring around the rim and a wooden plug at the pointed end.

"You should never deny any gods," he said. "We dwarfs know so much more about them than you. The farther we move from the haunts of men, the oftener we are able to surprise the gods and see and speak with them. Gods dwell in every spring, in every tree, in every branch of mistletoe on the lofty oaks. Gods dwell in the mead, in the cock that calls for the sunrise, in the fish that lies in the water below the fosse. Shepherds can tell you of good-natured Thor, who sits with his goats among the rocks. When he catches sight of us he angrily smites the rock with his hammer, so that the splinters fall about us, but we pick them up and keep them in our belt for a protection. Were we to pray to all the gods and think of contenting and gladdening them, there would never be time for aught else. Therefore we dwarfs have chosen the stone for our god, for in him slumbers what we love best: gold and silver. They are the noblest bowels of the stone. And now I ask you, stranger: is it not a fair thing to walk in a world where all things sing of godhead? Do you still smile at Jorgrimme's wisdom?"

"I still smile at Jorgrimme's wisdom," answered Folke Filbyter; "but if gold and silver are what you love most, maybe I am the man to reward a refreshing drink according to its worth. Speak out: what do you ask?"

"We dwarfs ask nothing, for whatever we ask, we never get so much as we desire. We ourselves silently settle what we hold to be just, and then see that it comes to us. When we stood on the grave-mound, I put a spell on you by tracing figures in the grass, that you might go astray and stop at last just by my hole. I knew that your lot and mine were to meet. Now take the horn and drink. It can be no more hazardous for you than for us, since you are no Christian. And now I will tell you a thing which you shall lay to your memory. There is a saying that if a Christian drinks from Månegarm he will long not only for the moon and the stars, but also for the invisible things behind them. And such a man will be terrible."

Folke Filbyter took the horn and emptied the bitter drink with zest. While he was doing so, the dwarf took a stone knife from his belt unobserved and cut a slit in the lower corner of the sack.

"Your juniper ale is good," said Folke Filbyter at last, "and I feel braced by it. Since you crave no reward, have thanks and farewell!"

He hunched the sack more easily on his back and continued his journey.

At last, through the fir-stems, there was a glimpse of open meadow land, and a lake bordered with reeds. Still farther in the distance lay cultivated fields with scattered dwellings, and he imagined the sack was getting lighter to carry.

On a slope overgrown with leafless oaks he discovered an abandoned shed without a door. There he sat to rest awhile on the threshold, which was as high as a bench.

As he was laying down the sack, his eyes stood perfectly still and he paled under the sunburn, seized with a fit of shivering. He saw that the sack had shrunk at one corner like a withered fruit. His finger found the slit through which a small part of the golden contents had already run out. He tied a knot over the slit and followed his tracks back to the cave, but it was empty. Only the ashes on the floor showed where the fire had been. With even heavier steps than when he had had the full load on his back, he returned after a while to the shed. He had found a few coins, but they were not many, and the snow was deep enough to hide the lost pieces for the dwarfs till the next thaw.

He sat upon the threshold, and the weather was clear. The stolid tenacity of his peasant's soul began by degrees to restore his wonted calm.

"Why should a homeless viking longer roam in search of land?" he exclaimed at last aloud, as though he wished every oak and every bush to hear him. "This place is fair and smiling. If I have sown the ground with coins of gold and silver, it is fitting I should stay and reap the crop myself. Here will I build me a home and it shall be called Folketuna. And you, Finn dwarfs, shall be my thralls."

III

Before he fetched fire from the neighbouring homesteads and began to clear his land, Folke Filbyter took care to have his title duly recognized. Five good witnesses went with him through the woods and set up his landmarks. He was so greedy of land that he did not despise the most worthless swamp. He paid for all in the presence of witnesses, and Ulf Ulfsson, the seller, at once melted down the silver into small bars and buried it in a place unknown.

In those days there were no poor men or beggars, either south of the forests or in the land of the Sveas. Those who owned nothing dwelt with richer men and were content. Therefore, in a district inhabited chiefly by wild hunters who worshipped Ti, the god of strife, an ancient law prevailed. according to this, he who took another man's goods by force might keep them; he who stole was to restore half; but he who begged was to lose his life. The spirit of this law prevailed also among the settled freeholders, but there was no lack of turbulent spirits. These were tempted by anything new, and especially by the rumours of Folke Filbyter's wealth. Therefore he had not long to wait for all the men he wanted. Some became his tenants on the forest land, but most were taken into his household as thralls, and at night a large body kept watch about the clearing-fires.

The mighty hall of Folketuna was soon roofed over, with fresh oak timbers fitted together and made tight with moss still green. Loud cracks were heard in the walls as the summer sun began to dry the wood. There were neither high-seat posts nor box-beds, neither skins nor cushions. The master of the house was content with a long bench by the hearth and a sheaf of straw on the smooth-trodden floor. His first care was to provide, not wall hangings or decorated bowls, but twelve white hens and a red cock. Then he bought goats and sheep. For all these fluttering and tramping animals he erected a partition in a corner, so that they might go freely in and out of the house. The door of the ante-room at the end was almost always ajar. It was so low that a man had to stoop to enter; and, if he was an enemy, his death-blow awaited him from the maple club which always lay upon the bench.

Little by little he filled his sheds and pens with red cattle and small shaggy horses. And never did a man put a milk bowl to his lips with more radiant health and contentment than he. His cheeks were rounder than those of a housewife who lingers too long in her dairy; his voice was deep and sombre like a giant's, and his hands looked capable of forcing open the jaws of a bear. Every morning as the red cock crew on the partition the master of Folketuna rose from his straw refreshed by sleep. His first steps were to the wolf-pit, but as he always found it empty he went on to his thralls in the fields. He held his great plough in such honour that no thrall was ever allowed to thrust it into the earth or to hold the handles. He milked his cows himself and rubbed down his horses and oxen, and he brought with him the smell of a herdsman when he came back to the hall.

He was never harsh with his thralls, for they were as the hair of his head and the skin of his arm. On the contrary, it was his pride to feed and clothe them well. Though they could scarcely have found a better master, they would have readily forgiven him for beating and starving them if only he had borne himself somewhat more proudly, marking the distance between himself and them. They would have liked him to hang bells on his horses, to line his walls with costly hangings and to spread a white cloth on his table and forbid them to eat at it. This would have given the place more splendour and consideration. As it was, when a stranger entered, his greeting was marred by a covert smile at the master of the house and his frugality in the midst of riches. This exasperated the thralls to such an extent that they were often sullen and unwilling; but then he gave them a taste of his peasant's tongue and showed himself as tough as bast and as immovable as a rock.

Now and then itinerant traders came with salt from Halland, the price of which had risen owing to the turbulent times. If it chanced that they travelled with more precious wares through the forests, he sent out his men to plunder them. In this way his wealth continually increased. The slain were thrown into a swamp, which thereafter he never ventured to pass except in broad daylight and with many attendants. Folke hated Thor and Frey and Odin and Christ with equal cordiality and believed in none of them. Nevertheless, if he found a thunderbolt lying in his field, he thrust it into his door-post as a protection against fire. And in secret, unseen by any of his thralls, he had a Christian man to pray over his great plough. He believed no more in the man than in the thunderbolt, but he considered that in such serious matters a good husbandman ought to take every precaution. Nor could he be deterred either by rain or snow from setting out on Thor's day with all his household to sacrifice. On that day he went to one of the little round shrines built of stakes which stood under the oaks by the roadside with collapsed birch-bark roof and moss-grown image. If threatening omens appeared in the entrails of the victim, he was seized with such superstitious terror that he caused torches to be burnt all night and posted guards. But hardly had the first light of dawn appeared above the smoke-hole, when he became as bold and confident as before, until the next week.

All this the thralls could see through, and they tried to obey him submissively, but they had no respect for him.

One morning, when he made his usual visit to the wolf-pit, he threw his spade on his shoulder. The thralls were cutting grass, and he said to them:

"Great and fair is my Folketuna, rich and fertile is the soil, all yields well. The wolf-pit alone has never given me anything, either a skin for the winter or game for the spit. Therefore I think it well to fill it in. What say you, children?"

"We say," answered the bailiff, who was foreman of the thralls, "that it would be unwisely done. An empty strand may one day show the finest mussel."

The dairymaid, who was at the head of the women thralls and carried the keys of the pantry, would also have said something, but hesitated. Only when she saw her master look specially at her did she say:

"You can see even from here that the sprigs spread over the pits have been disturbed. To-day you will find a quarry. But I tell you, master, if it is a fine mussel, beware lest it cut your fingers."

He had not expected this, and, warned by her words, he raised his spade like an ax and crept forward.

As soon as he had bent over the pit and pushed aside the twigs, he dropped the spade again. His easy gaiety welled up in his soul like fermenting wine, till his whole face turned red as blood.

"By the bandy-legged Asa Thor," he cried, "when did a man find such game in his wolf-pit?"

Then he stood silent and motionless longer than the thralls had ever seen him. It was now full summer. Heavy bumble-bees buzzed in the air. Wild camomile and orchis bloomed in the yard, and in the fields the corn was already yellowed. Over on the lake a fisherman rocked in his punt, and it was still black from the fire that had hollowed it out.

One by one the thralls came up to the pit and stood in a ring. Only the dairymaid, who had already glanced down through the boughs, kept a little behind the others. Down at the bottom sat a little Finn maiden, raising her hands in fear and supplication. Although she was wrapped to the cheeks in ample foxes' skins, he recognized her at once. He was not mistaken: she was one of the dwarf's daughters who had danced within the mound, though she had then worn nothing but the fur socks and the dangling chains of glass beads. The chains were now wound about her neck and sparkled against the furs like rain. Her eyes, which then were wild and seemed filled with blood, now burned deep and calm as two brown lakes, but they were the same. Once since, he had dreamt of her, and in his dream she had sat cracking her glass beads like nuts, and now out of each crept a little black worm with horns.

"Now I look closely," he said, "I see in your belt a whole row of the coins I lost in the snow. You dwarfs cannot accuse me of haste in avenging myself on you. Tell me, how did you come here?"

"Wandering alone, I lost my way in the darkness," she wailed, smacking her tongue and talking with her thumbs in the manner of Finns. "None had ears when the wild man's daughter called. None helped her when she fell into the trap, and she was too small to pull herself out."

The dairywoman came a little nearer.

"She is fair and shapely enough, the little one, but you must not listen to her, master. When one of her people sees a red fox he calls it white, just because a dwarf can never speak the truth. Be sure there is some plot in this. I have heard much ill of Jorgrimme and his hole. Were he honestly inclined, he would come himself to your gate with his daughters and ask you to buy them. If you receive her into your household, much evil may come of it."

He thrust his spade into the ground and began to reflect. "Think you, then," he asked at length, "that I am to sit alone all my days with no other delight for my eyes than your grimy faces?"

"As for us thralls," she answered, "I know of udalmen of higher birth than you have not disdained to place thrall women beside them on their couches. I have been in houses where every bondwoman carried a bag on her back, and in every bag there screamed a child. That is the custom here south of the forests."

"In my house the women thralls must be content with straw."

"All we meant was that you should let her stay in the pit, where nobody need touch her. If she wishes to get out, be sure she knows runes which will help her as well as any ladder. And then we thought you should have more care for the honour of your house. You are already past middle age, and so rich a franklin as you has only to drive to his nearest neighbour to make a good marriage bargain."

He turned his back on her and began to walk across the field. When the thralls saw that, they followed and took up their work again. Meanwhile he muttered to himself:

"Well do I know the proud franklin's daughters, who bring in their brothers to sit in the hall, and who strike at their husbands with their bunch of keys."

When some time had passed and dinner was ready, he returned to the hall. He was thinking of the dwarf girl and remembered her as he had seen her in his dream when she was dancing. But at the same time he was thinking of something very different which really occupied him more, and this was that the thralls were growing insolent and wanted to give him advice. This was his reward for being a good master and promising them new homespun clothes every second autumn. This made him obstinately hold his peace, and again he was tough as bast.   However, when he saw that the thralls did not come in at once but took their spades and shuffled off in a grey crowd to the wolf-pit, he called to the bailiff.

"We think it best to fill in the pit again, so she can stay there, said the bailiff, halting for a moment.   "The only thing is all the gold and silver she has on her belt, but we can get that next summer and bring it to you."

Folke Filbyter seated himself on the bench, where the porridge-bowl already stood steaming.   He filled his spoon and blew upon it, and through the door he watched the thralls taking their stand around the pit.   They were waiting for the bailiff, and when at last he came up leisurely, they consulted awhile, going first to one side, then to the other, and looking down into the pit.   The bailiff seemed trying to persuade them to wait a little and not let their food get cold, for he pointed to the house; but they were impatient and uneasy.

"What evil have I done you, that you should treat me so ill?" the dwarf girl complained.   "Run to my father in the wood.   He will give you much silver for my life.   Stone Eye, Stone Brow, God of the Fosse, Umasumbla, help me!"

"No stone god can help you any more," scoffed the bailiff almost good-humouredly.   "But shut your eyes and lean a little forward, then it will be over all the sooner."

The thralls pulled aside the boughs.   Their backs, already bent, were bowed yet deeper and their leather aprons flapped loudly.   A faint weeping was the only other sound, as their spades threw earth and sand into the pit, which had been dug for the wolves of the wilderness but not for this unhappy daughter.

IV

FOLKE FILBYTER took his time, the better to show his will and his power. He waited till he had eaten his fill, then thrust the bowl from him and went to the wolf-pit. "We are filling up the pit for our own sakes, but still more for yours, master," said the bailiff, fingering the whip at his belt. "You will be pleased with us afterwards."

Folke Filbyter gave him no answer. When he leaned over he saw that she still had her head free and was holding up one hand as though appealing for help to the last. He took a firm hold of her arm and pulled her up into the sunlight. Her skin was so hot that he could feel it burn his hand. Without letting go he carried her like a doll straight into the hall and set her down in the straw.

Then he went to the corner and opened the chest. It had many padlocks and bolts and was weighted besides with stones chained to the corners, so that the strength of many men would be required to move it from its place. There was a jingling of jewels and silver ingots as he plunged his hand into the chest, turning them over without making up his mind. Then he brought out a chain of gold and threw it over the beam that crossed the hall, two paces from the hearth. It was a chain of fine rings and had many pearls great and small. The clasp gleamed brightly with a calm bluish light like an evening star. "What is your name?" he asked.

"I am called Jorgrimme's daughter."

He patted her on the cap.

"Be not sad, little dwarf girl," he said; "you shall stay with me at Folketuna and never more need to scrape a fox's skin for your clothing. Every day you shall look upon that gold chain while you were about your housework. It shall be the last thing your brown eyes shall see when they fall asleep and the first when they wake. And if you turn out to my liking, you may take down the chain from the beam and wear it for your own."

Then the dwarf maiden dried her tears and began to feel at home, so that she scarcely ever left the place to visit her own people in the woods. Only on clear starlight nights did she sometimes steal away to her sister to dance and read the future. And then she always managed by guile or by fair words to bring back with her some of the coins that had fallen from Folke Filbyter's sack and that the dwarfs had picked up on the melting of the snow. The people of Folketuna therefore began little by little to put up with her presence, since she brought wealth to the house and was never in bad humour. The yard before the house was surrounded by a fence, and at last Jorgrimme and his other daughter used to steal up to the gate fairly often. They stood there with their heads over the gate-posts asking for the loan of a kettle or offering to barter some game for a piece of homespun cloth. She would then lay what they asked for on the grass and go back into the hall with all the thralls and shut the door. The dwarfs made haste to complete the transaction and then ran into the woods. But sometimes, when Folke Filbyter wanted to amuse himself, he stood at the window and shot arrows after them.

Next summer she bore him a son. Then Folke Filbyter lifted her from the floor and carried her to the gold chain, that she might take it herself from the beam. After that she lay in the straw playing with her baby and the jewel, and the very next day she was back minding the kettle on the hearth. Her place was among the thralls, for she wore neither keys nor cloak like a lawfully bought udalwoman. Nor did she suckle the boy, but now and then put a little marrow into his mouth and then let him lie.

The boy was given the name of Ingemund. She then gave birth to Hallsten, and the third summer to Ingevald.

She often took the children in a bag on her back when she roamed the woods. They soon learned to race the wolf with ski on their feet and to hit him over the back with the staff. When they were half grown up, their father sent for them. Seated on the bench, he asked them whether they would cast lots for the inheritance of Folketuna or would take service in the king's body-guard like the sons of other rich franklins. He did this only to try them. Ingemund and Hallsten showed him that they had already shafted three dozen arrows apiece and that they could fling the club right through the hall and out upon the grass. Ingevald, the youngest, was not so active and had no accomplishment to show beyond being quick of speech and able to answer any riddle.

"Well, then," said Folke Filbyter to his sons, "you, Ingevald, who are youngest and weakest, shall stay under my correction so long as I live. But in return you alone shall inherit the whole of Folketuna. You others for your share shall receive at once from my chest enough to pay the hire of fifty men and to buy yourselves good coats of mail and weapons. My ship Menglöd and two other ships of mine still lie on the beach by the shield maiden's mound. You shall take them. They are built of oak and well covered over, and you shall take with you tools and timber to repair them. No advice for the conduct of life have I to give you, for I am an ignorant man and have not the gift of words. Nor can I commend you to any gods, for you will find many of all sorts, and they will all fail you when your own arm fails. But if I sit in my mound when you return, you shall shame to set foot on it if you come to beg."

Ingemund and Hallsten then went off a-viking to the East, but Ingevald stayed at home among the thralls. He was his mother's darling. She dressed him out in bright patchwork clothes after the fancy of the dwarf folk, but he went to work with the thralls and cut stakes and stripped withies like the rest. In the evening he crept in among them as they sat about the hearth twining bast or carding wool, and learned to imitate their heavy, drawling speech. He remained a thrall in all his ideas, for he knew nothing of the world beyond what was known to the thralls.

It was Folke Filbyter's delight to hold weddings among his thralls. What he liked best was to marry a young serving-man to one of the oldest and most shrivelled of the women. Now he had a bondwoman whom he called Tova Lie-a-bed, because she was old and worn out and lay sighing most of the day in the straw. One day when time was heavy on his hands he got up a wedding between her and a young thrall who was called Calf. The bailiff drove in all the servants and lined them up with wisps of straw under the arms, as was the custom when they were to dance at a wedding. He was indulgent with them when they were at work, trying to imitate his master; but when they were at play they were so dull that he had to take his whip and crack it about their broad heels and flat feet.

"Tova, Tova!" cried Folke Filbyter, laughing till he could not see. "Do you think we shall let you lie in the sheep-fold with the ram when your bridal straw is ready? Into the dance with you, like a good girl! No, wait a bit, Tova! Tell us first whether it is true that when you were young and foolish you were snatched from ship to ship for the sake of your white arms."

She passed her thick and crooked fingers over her forehead and found herself in the middle of the ring, completely flustered. This prompted her master to carry on the joke with greater zest. "You are too modest to answer such questions, little Tova. And you are afraid of your bridegroom's wrath. He is so young and fiery, your bridegroom. But tell us, at any rate, whether it is true that you are the daughter of a great and powerful chieftain in Friesland?"

"I don't remember him," she answered in a slow drawl. "But I remember a young woman, my mother, who sat in the narrow castle-window and plucked me cherries from the tree-tops."

"Didn't I know it was true! You have got a noble bride, Calf, and you will find her quiet and docile. Now lively with your feet! Wake them up a little, bailiff! Cut at the bridegroom's heels! That's the way!"

Ingevald kept as far off as possible, hiding among the bashful ones who could not be made to come forward. Some of them were so accustomed to work that they were tired of standing with idle hands. They began to sweep the corners and hoist the kettle as they looked on. The hens ran cackling along the sides of the hall, and sticks, bits of bark and chips of straw whirled in the air, while the dancers circled round in the thick smoke. The feeble daylight fell now and again on sulky, hard-set faces and vanished in an instant.

The dairywoman had already poured out the honey porridge and set it on the bench before Folke Filbyter. She was drying the horn to go and fetch beer from the brewhouse, when the bailiff elbowed his way with leisurely good humour through the dancers and signed to the thralls to stop, by holding his whip upside down.

"Master," he said, "some strange ox has come into the fields, for our oxen are bellowing in their stalls."

"You are right," replied Folke Filbyter, pointing to the door, where a wagon painted blue had halted.

It was drawn by a well-groomed ox with silky hide, the reins were decorated with tassels, the yoke was carved with roses and leaves in all the hues of summer and hung with countless little jingling bells. The man who threw down the reins and alighted had his legs swathed to the knee in crossed bands. A venerable grey beard covered his whole chest, but his bright, shrewd eyes came in view only when he bent down in the low doorway and looked in surprise into the hall. The fowls met him on the threshold and fluttered back, scattering themselves again along the walls in a run, and the thralls stood stock-still with their wisps of straw, not having the sense to make way. It evidently took him a while to accustom himself to the smoke sufficiently to discover Folke Filbyter, who was still seated on the bench with the porridge-bowl between his knees.

"Ulf Ulfsson, your neighbour, greets the master of the house," he began. Instead of the scornful smile with which other strangers entered Folketuna, he stopped with a frown on his brow some paces from the bench. "Maybe you remember that it was from me you bought a great part of your broad land. Since then we have not seen each other. And now I will give you an easy riddle to read, Folke Filbyter. Tell me who is the man who ought to be feared like a bear and honoured like an udalman, but is frowned upon and laughed at by all."

Folke Filbyter thrust his spoon deep into his porridge. "Ingevald, Ingevald, my son," he said, "come here and show that you are quick of tongue and have your mother's head. Your father has no skill in riddles. Now leave your drawling which you use among the thralls. Come forward boldly, Ingevald! Tell me the man who ought to be feared like a bear and honoured like an udalman, but is frowned upon and laughed at by all."

Ingevald rubbed his shoulder against the wall in rustic awkwardness, but then plucked up courage. He had lively brown eyes and his mother's sallow complexion. He wore silver rings in his ears, a number of red and yellow patches were sewed on his clothes, and with all his bashfulness he felt flattered and happy at being the object of attention. He advanced, a slight and tawdry figure, to the hearth, and answered boldly:

"It is Ulf Ulfsson, who comes uninvited to a wedding just as the feast is beginning."

Ulf Ulfsson bit his lip.

"A good riddle may have more than one answer," he said. "If I am insulted in your house, Folke Filbyter, I must put up with it. It was not to do you honour I came. And it is not easy to guess that a wedding is in progress here. I see no green boughs in the corners, no flowers on the floor, though 'tis true I stumble over chips and bark in the holes in it. Your roof-beams are black and sooty underneath, but above they are whitened with the fowls' droppings. And I have been told that the wedding-hall should be decked with blue hangings, but the half-rotten calf-skins you have drying on your walls give out such a stench as cures hunger and thirst at once. Here you sit making sport with your thralls and thinking of naught else, and yet you are a man of wealth and might take the lead in the hundred. It was you I meant by my riddle, though I have to tell it you myself. There is not a huckster who would not laugh in your face to see you puffing over your porridge."

Folke Filbyter stared at him and felt his words filling his ears and brain, but he did not understand them. There was in him a broad underlying gentleness, though no one had taught him the use of gifts which seemed to him suspicious, and it caused him a confusion akin to modesty if they were ever observed. All he understood was that he was the best of masters, but he nevertheless had a feeling that Ulf Ulfsson was his superior in every way—and he was not pleased to see him.

Ulf Ulfsson kept at a distance.

"Why do you never come to the Thing like other udalmen?" he asked. "We need men. Or have you not heard that when old King Emund had been laid in his mound, his earl Stenkil came into power? When he presides at the winter sacrifice at Upsala, he does not drink to the memory of the gods, but looks down and whispers to his Christian body-guard."

"Stenkil does not shear my sheep," answered Folke Filbyter, "nor does he shoe my horses. Here at Folketuna I am master, and not the miserable upstart race of earls that threatens

Upsala temple. Have you any news of greater import than this, Ulf Ulfsson?"

"I have."

"Then say it out, for I know not many things that can fright me."

"Well, then, you shall hear my news. Yesterday there came among us the first beggar."

"I do not understand you, Ulf Ulfsson."

"Yesterday there came for the first time a man who wanders around asking for gifts of charity."

Folke Filbyter stood up, blazing with anger.

"It is a disgrace to hear of such things. Lend me the vaga-bond. I'll take him into the fields and harness him to the plough. Is his master too bad and niggardly to feed and clothe him?"

"That you may ask him yourself when he comes, if you care to bandy words with a beggar. But bear in mind that he who slays a foreign priest must make atonement as for a countryman. Thus does our law even now protect the Christians. He is on his way hither, and I have made all haste to be here before him and warn you. You need not think I did it for your sake; you are not likely to stuff this scrip with many gifts. But I will tell you frankly that in bad times like these we two must think of standing side by side, though neither of us likes the other. And if my eyes are not mistaken, this is he approaching over the meadow."

All turned again to the door. In the sunshine came an old man with a knotted staff in one hand and a little bag in the other. He wore a coarse rope about his waist and was bare-footed, and he walked in haste, as though he saw a long road before him and feared any needless delay. On arriving at the door, he spread out his arms with an unpretending gesture and said in a low voice:

"For Jesus Christ's sake, give me alms. My name is Jakob. Has no one told you of old Jakob? It is not for myself I beg, but for my good Master. I thank you humbly for the smallest gift; but if you are rich, franklin, then give a tithe, and if you are just, give all."

"Ingevald, my son," said Folke Filbyter, and his voice was choked with rising anger, "here it is not the custom to give but to take, for this is my land. Take the bag from the old man. Then give him two strokes with his own staff, one for himself, the other for his master, who feeds and clothes him so ill that he has to beg."

Ingevald went out and snatched the old man's scrip. In it were some coins and finger-rings and a piece of dry bread. He let him keep the bread, but tied the scrip fast to his own belt. Then he lustily gave him the first stroke over the back as hard as he could. But when he came to deal the second blow it was weaker and gentler. He was in two minds about it, for the old man took him round the neck and kissed him on both temples.

"I thank you, my dear child, for letting me suffer for my dear Master's sake," he said. "And I thank and bless you all, for none can love you more truly than I, my dear, dear brethren. I had thought to tarry awhile among you and tell you of my Master, but I see that to-day you would not listen to me. I must choose a better time."

Thereupon he at once resumed his journey with the same eager haste, and his eyes, which had moistened from the pain, shone as with the deepest joy.

"They are dangerous people, those!" muttered Ulf Ulfsson, dropping his eyes and stroking his beard. Folke Filbyter still understood nothing of it, but raised his voice with more authority than before.

"Come here, Ingevald! You did your duty well, and now you shall stand before Ulf Ulfsson that he may take you by the hand. Have no fear, Ingevald; he is our neighbour and wishes you no harm. Come here now, I will take you to him myself. He used harsh words like all great franklins, but now I begin to guess his meaning. There is need of men at the Thing. But I am not a man of words, and long have I sat in silence. My coat of mail is rusted together and I can no longer shake it out. You shall have weapons and a new byrnie, Ingevald, and you shall go to the Thing in my stead."

He pushed his son forward, but Ulf Ulfsson, who had not forgotten the boy's sharp answer to his riddle, passed his hand scornfully over his wiry hair and gave him a smack on the cheek.

"Look," he said, "your son has horse's hair and his cheek is so lathery that it cannot blush even for a blow. These are signs of Finn blood. A Finn dwarf cannot blush, however

you may pinch him or strike him in the face or abuse him.
Not many of the free men at the Thing would listen to such a
one, even if you went with him yourself and owned him for
your son. It would have been better had you turned out that
child into the woods in time. Why, man, is it with such
offspring that you think to found a house and a family?"

Folke Filbyter seized him by the cloak. Such an insult before all his household was a thing he had never known, and
Ulf Ulfsson's calm and haughty scorn confused and silenced
him. The wealthy master of Folketuna began to stammer, and
Ingevald whispered to him:

"Father, let me go and bolt the door while you strike him
down. Then the bailiff and I will carry him out to the swamp."

"I have good ears," Ulf Ulfsson went on. "And I know
well that if I accuse you before the Thing and have your
swamp dug, you will be in a bad case. Nor would I hesitate
a single day if prudence did not tell me that we franklins and
neighbours must now make common cause against the Christians."

Folke Filbyter came to his senses and dropped the cloak.

"You are unarmed, Ulf Ulfsson, and you are under my roof.
If you think of parting from me with an insult, I promise
you your house shall burn this very night. But if you were
in earnest in desiring to see a change at Folketuna and fellowship between us, then you will drive me in your own wagon
to the richest house in all the hundred. And there you will
be spokesman for my son, that he may make a good marriage.
I myself have long had it in my mind that things cannot go
on as hitherto. For my part it is no matter, but Ingevald is
growing up and he will have a great heritage. If you accept
my conditions, lend me your blue cloak. My grey homespun
is no wedding-garment. I would fain see the franklin that
can refuse when Folke Filbyter seeks a wife for his son by the
dwarf woman!"

"The richest house in the hundred, next to Folketuna, is
mine."

Folke Filbyter gave a start, as though a secret door had
suddenly sprung open disclosing a stair of which he had
had no inkling. He was not clever enough to dissemble the new
ideas that suddenly crossed his mind. He felt that in an instant the tables had been turned and that now it was he who had

to speak and give advice. With a side-glance, offensive in its distrust, he dropped his voice and whispered:

"Neighbour, you have more business at heart than you have yet disclosed."

With that he clapped Ulf Ulfsson on the shoulder, but once more he started in surprise before the sombre gravity that his words called forth on the face of his guest.

"My business I have already told you," Ulf Ulfsson answered at last, after a long silence, as though he would have avoided any confession. "Nevertheless I cannot deny that on my way hither many thoughts came to my mind. I knew but little of how you kept house within doors. As I halted at the landmark between our properties and watered my ox in the brook, I thought to myself that perhaps you had children as I have and that a marriage might be the best assurance of a league between our houses."

"Now you speak honestly, Ulf Ulfsson."

"And shall continue. When I met you in your hall and saw your son, these thoughts were quickly blown to the winds. Your son is base-born, and I hold my daughter too good to amend the blood of your race."

"The days are long for a maiden who sits waiting for a suitor, dear neighbour, and you must not be hard on her. Here your daughter will be well treated. She shall live with me and share my table and cloth."

"I have not yet seen a cloth in your house, Folke Filbyter, and my daughter is well off where she is, in my hands. Your Folketuna knows nothing of good manners. Your thralls stare as though they had never before seen a well-clad man."

"Do you know that I was once a chief and had three ships at sea?"

Ulf Ulfsson smiled.

"It sounds like a tale, but I have heard it is true."

"The first beggar has come to these parts to-day, Ulf Ulfsson. You have just told me what such birds of passage portend. Choose now whether you will have league or strife between our houses."

Ulf Ulfsson turned aside to go, but controlled himself.

"The decision does not rest with me alone," he answered reluctantly.

"Then you have grown-up sons?"

"They will be hard nuts to crack at a betrothal. But you must not think I am overweening because I come of an old Lawman family.[7] Who can say whether your narrow-shouldered son's gaudy rags may not please my child better than they please me? I have set foot beneath your roof, and now you have the right to enter my house. There you can put what questions you wish. If you choose to expose yourself to a refusal and perhaps a sneer, it is your affair. The times are so threatening that I should drive home with a more cheerful mind if I were sure of a wise decision. Friends we shall never be, but it is my desire that at least we shall never be enemies. Here is my cloak; did you not ask the loan of it?"

Folke Filbyter wrapped the cloak around him and fastened the clasp. He went to his chest in the corner and took out a bass-wood box. In it lay a little crown, the golden oak-leaves of which were soft and flexible like those of a natural wreath. The thralls had never seen anything so splendid; they stretched over each other's shoulders to get a better view of it, and at that moment they felt for the first time a real respect for their master.

"She shall have this," he said, "and a silver-embroidered fillet and a finger-ring of gold and a mantle with sleeves and a key-ring . . . and a milk-white palfrey to ride. You shall see, Ulf Ulfsson, that I can bid high!"

Ulf Ulfsson had a preoccupied air as he helped him into the wagon, where there was little room for so burly a passenger. Folke Filbyter held the box on his knee, and as the wagon drove away the thralls heard him raising his offers.

"Two silver spoons she shall have," he cried, "and two hundred ells of homespun and twenty ells of linen . . . and a kerchief, and a mattress stuffed with down . . . and cushions embroidered in gold . . . and fifty marks of pure silver with the stamp of a Flemish town! And each of her brothers shall have a shirt with silver buttons . . . and for yourself you shall have as much threshed grain as two pair of oxen can draw in two journeys! Let me see who will say no, by the bandy-legged, hunchbacked Asa Thor!"

[7] The Lawman was the elected president of the provincial Assembly or Thing. He represented the whole body of landowners and was held in high honour.

V

THERE was silence in the house when the wagon had rumbled off. By once more holding his whip aloft with the butt-end upward, the bailiff gave the thralls to understand that they were free for the evening. They shuffled out in a crowd of grey figures.

Ingevald stayed behind at the door. The insult that had been put upon him burned itself into his mind with a pain that seemed past remedy. All at once it had opened his eyes so that he saw the dirt and the untidiness of the hall. For the first time he noticed the rank smell of the hides on the walls. He saw with painful clearness how rude and undignified had been his father's behaviour when he drove away boasting loudly beside the grave Ulf Ulfsson. Ingevald had never heard any such proud and manly speech as Ulf Ulfsson's, and he had listened eagerly to every word he uttered. And he felt pangs of remorse at the thought of old Jakob whom he had beaten. He could still feel his cold lips on his temples.

He ran out to follow the thralls, as usual, but could not find them. What was it they had been whispering as they passed him? Another thing that surprised him was that Tova had not crawled back into the sheep-fold in the corner, but had gone out with the others. "Ingevald!" called a drawling voice from the cattle-sheds, but, when he came there, he found nobody. The cattle were at pasture, and he went through the empty stalls, which were full of cobwebs. "Ingevald!" called another thrall's voice far away on the other side of the house, but he could find nobody there either. It dawned on him that the thralls had stolen away and were trying to mislead him by calling in different directions. Had he fallen into such contempt that even the thralls hid from him? Was it his fault that his mother was not a free udalwoman?

Search as he might, he could find no one. The narrow-shouldered, tawdry son and heir to the whole of this rich estate stood solitary among the wheel-ruts in the trampled grass, and on the dragon's head of the gable-end sat the magpies laughing at the desertion of Folketuna.

Then he called to mind that several of the thralls had lately stolen out at night. Among the others there had been whispering and sometimes sobs, but they had always checked themselves and feigned to be asleep as soon as he sat up in the straw. There was something they wished to conceal from him. He pondered over it in the bitterness he now felt towards everyone, himself included.

He began to walk aimlessly towards the woods, merely to stifle the sobs that convulsed his throat. The summer evening was fine and still and the oaks seemed huger in their immobility. More busily than the bees, the furry drones hummed a while in the air before creeping into their mossy nests. Without thinking, he stood a long time watching a squirrel, which put its head out of the window of its house to observe the weather. On finding it clear and without a vestige of a storm-cloud, the little weather-prophet removed the plug from his door and began to throw out nutshells on to the shrine at the bottom of the tree. Their clattering on the ragged birch-bark roof roused Ingevald, and he turned away to avoid seeing the image in the shrine. He did this partly from fear, but still more from shame. He felt he belonged no more to the race protected by the gods of the silvan temples.

Close by the path lay a source, renowned for its good watersprite, the friend of man. He used often to sit there gazing in self-love at his gaudy clothes and big silver ear-rings. If he looked long into the clear water, he sometimes thought he could discern the pale face of the beautiful nymph, and then he was seized with a wild desire to throw himself into her arms. But now, when he bent over the source, he saw himself with the eyes of Ulf Ulfsson.

"Look," he sobbed, "my cheek is like leather. However hard I pinch it or strike it, it cannot blush. And my hair is wiry like horsehair. Never can I take my place at the Thing among the free-born udalmen. If I go there, no one will listen to me. And all will laugh at my patchwork clothes."

He tore at his motley jerkin and spat contemptuously at his own image in the spring.

Still driven on by mocking visions, it was to the Thing-stead and nowhere else that he directed his steps with ever-increasing haste. He muttered that if he might never stand there among other men, he would at least tell the dumb judgment-stones of his misfortunes.

By degrees the oak-forest grew thinner and gave place to cultivated land, which in the distance was bordered by dark ridges. Where the fields began was the Thing-mound. To his astonishment he found a crowd of people within the circle of huge stones. Accustomed to the feelings of a thrall, his first thought was to hide, as though he had no business there. He crouched behind a bush. But soon he discovered that there were no blue coats among the assembly, only the grey homespun of the thralls. He recognized several of those who had stolen from his father's house, and by one of the stones sat the weary Tova, sighing as usual. So it was to hold a secret thrall-thing in the dusk that they had stayed out at nights? And the speaker, who stood in the middle addressing them, was old Jakob with his staff. When from time to time he clasped his hands and asked for silence, all was perfectly still, and the grasshoppers sang in the dewy, fragrant grass.

Ingevald heard the low-voiced preacher turn at last to Tova and ask her what she thought of death.

"We thralls have no thoughts about it," she answered. "Thor and Frey despise us, and the One-Eyed at the fosse is the god of the Finn dwarfs. All I know, Jakob, is that it gives me great comfort to hear you."

"Then, Tova, I have understood better than you what Jakob has told us," said the bailiff, who stood beside her and still carried his whip in his belt. "Now we thralls have got a god of our own."

"'Tis true, 'tis true," repeated Jakob. "I have told you of Him that you may be of good heart and wait and not revolt against your masters when one day they shall order you to worship the new God. The king no longer takes pleasure in the heathen sacrifices of Upsala, but chooses rather to dwell beside my brethren at Skara. Hundreds of chiefs and thanes assemble there every Easter and Midsummer to receive baptism. Patience, patience and longing, that is your heritage, but hereafter it shall be a glorious one. Now I will give each of you a pinch of salt, so far as the salt in my scrip will last. I conjure thee, essence of salt, flame of wisdom, that thy mysterious force be a wholesome means to the expulsion of all evil! I conjure thee, by the new God and the love of His Son! And now I will approach so many of you as I can, and breathe upon your faces. Depart, thou Prince of Darkness, thou Devil, from these bodies which I dedicate as the abodes of the Lord God. With the sign of the Cross I mark you with soot and salt between your eyebrows, that Satan may be affrighted if he return to creep again into your entrails. Simply, as I have been taught, I consecrate you all, both those who are nearest and those who lie concealed behind stones and bushes. I bless you and consecrate you as instruments of God's love."

Jakob laid his hands on Tova and the bailiff and prayed at great length. Then he kissed those who stood nearest and took up his beggar's scrip and resumed his hurried wandering. The thralls felt proud and strengthened, believing that it was the sign of Thor's hammer he had drawn on their brows. But what surprised them most was to hear him return thanks for the blows he had received at savage Folketuna.

"Can he be a thrall like ourselves?" they asked one another as they separated to steal home.

"I spy red rags behind the junipers," a woman whispered. "It must be the son of Folketuna. Has he been listening too?"

"I shall not betray you," answered Ingevald between his teeth. "Now I have learnt where my god is to be found. I shall go to him. Upon the rock by the fosse stands the god of the dwarfs. There stands the One-Eyed, and him I can strike and ill-use without even a thrall taking pity on him."

He could hear that someone was following him with padded, tripping steps, but he did not look round. He turned aside through the heather under the firs. Notches in the bark, nearly grown over, showed him he was on the right path, but it was late and he had to stop now and then to make them out. When he did so, the steps behind him ceased.

His jerkin caught in the twigs again and again, and it gave him pleasure to pull it away sharply, so that some of the patches were torn off and hung on the trees and bushes. Soon the roar of the fall told him that he could no longer lose his way.

A beaten path led him on, for here lay Jorgrimme's cave, and farther on, behind a heap of stones, the spray was whirling.

There stood the god on a shelf of rock, casting no shadow in the twilight. Raised upon four smaller stones, he was of no very imposing size, and he grew narrower towards the top like a pestle. In the middle of the block a dark hole gaped, as though made by a giant's finger, and this was the dreaded eye.

Ingevald leaned his elbow on the god and looked down into the fosse. He still noticed that he was not alone. The crumbling, moss-grown bones and horns of victims, which lay scattered over the rocks, crackled in his rear like trampled twigs. And he knew who it was: from the first he had guessed that it was his mother who was following him.

By bending his head a little to one side, he was able to recognize her. She stopped on the edge of the cliff a little way from him and looked down into the same brown stream, which turned white only where foamed above the eddies. For a long time they stood thus, as though unaware of each other's presence. Never before had it struck him how small she was and how prematurely old and repulsively ugly. Can it be she who brought me into the world? he thought.

"Ingevald," she said at last, "I was among the rest of the thralls and I heard what you muttered between your teeth. That is why I have come after you."

"You are afraid I shall flog Umasumbla, the stone god?"

"No, I feared you would not have the courage for it. Take your revenge, my son. Revenge is the world's balm and delight. And then learn to love all that is of gold and silver. Nothing else is worth a day's toil."

She came a little nearer. When she stood close to him, chewing fern-root and smacking her tongue and talking with her thumbs, he conceived such disgust of her that he could no longer call her mother.

"I know well," she said with a quiver in her voice, "that to-night you have borrowed Ulf Ulfsson's eyes and it is with them you look upon me. Better were it if they burned like a true wolf's. Does not your cheek still smart from his blow? Not an hour longer will I stay with a master who lets us swallow such an insult without avenging it. I should poison him or stab him in his sleep."

"Then go! Go home to Jorgrimme's hole!"

"Jorgrimme is dead. On this rock he offered up my sister to the One-Eyed to prolong his life. But from that hour he lost all comfort and gladness. Then he went into the mound and stabbed himself with his stone knife. And when I came and found him dead, I placed his fishing-tackle and his pots about him and laid the horn Månegarm in his stiff hands. Then I covered the entrance with earth and turves. The elk grazes above his head. No one shall find the way thither, even as he himself knew not whence he came. Aye, go, go, dwarf woman! It is said that you are descended from chiefs of old who dwelt in the far North, where the women have beards and hunt the bison with bow and arrows and overcome the giants with their incantations. There lay boundless wastes full of snow and game, and there the dwarfs held sway. Alas, they are now few and poor! Now we hear but rarely of a dwarf being seen in the forests, and in these parts we were the last. Aye, go, go, dwarf woman, day and night; yet you will not meet your fellows. And when the dwarfs cease talking, they soon forget all words and can but howl and shriek with the storm."

"Aye, go, go!" he repeated bitterly. "Wade over the stream below the last fall. There all paths come to an end. There the wilderness begins. Why did you give me life if you dare not take it from me again? A thrall may buy his freedom and be as good a man as any, but how shall I ever free myself from all the evil I have inherited from you? My brothers knew what they were about when they hid themselves in distant lands. What will become of Folke Filbyter's house? Neither eagles nor doves can issue from a mole-hill. Men come to sell us salt, and spit upon the threshold. And if I shave my head and paint my cheeks, your blood will still flow in my veins. Can anyone be so luckless? Stone God, Stone Brow, Umasumbla, God of the Fosse, help us!"

With a roar of laughter he threw his arms around the stone god and lifted him. He did not know whence he derived such strength. With a shower of sparks and a roar like thunder, the One-Eyed plunged from his throne and rolled into the fosse. There he lay face downward, drenched in the spray, henceforth not to be distinguished from other stones.

"Dwarf child! dwarf child!" cried the mother in a shout of triumph. "That was my blood in your arms. Now I know that the flame of revenge lives in you. Why did I never make you drink from Månegarm? Why did I leave the horn with the dead who has no thirst? We must tear up the mound, Ingevald. We must plunder Jorgrimme in his grave and take from him his treasure. You see, all men have longings, but they lie in their cradles like good little children and smile without knowing what they want. But I shall offer you such a drink that these little children will rise from their cradles like wolfhounds and at last will swallow both stars and moon. And were you a Christian, you should even desire the invisible that is beyond all things. Show me your hands, that I may see whether your nails are sharp enough for digging. And tell me whether you will."

"I will!" he answered.

She took him by the wrist and they ran through the bracken to Jorgrimme's cave. They tore off the turves and the earth and the bark and crawled in to him.

"Jorgrimme!" she called into the dead man's ear. "You sit here among your pots and fishing-tackle, but we have come to take from you your dearest possession."

Jorgrimme was stiff and dry, and when she let go of him, he fell against the wall. There he lay with his knees drawn up and his hands around Månegarm. Then she took the horn from him, filled it from the pitcher, and drank, handing it afterwards to her son. Time after time she filled it till it ran over.

"The drink is soured and musty, but I am thirsty," he said.

Then she filled it for the last time with the dregs of the pitcher.

"Jorgrimme!" she cried. "You still sit there reaching out your hands, but they have nothing to take hold of! We have taken the horn from you!"

She moved her lips to form more words, but they would no longer obey her and madness was kindled in her eyes. It was the madness that always lurked in the soul of the dwarfs but, instead of making them dull and melancholy, took the form of a happy relief and boundless joy. This madness freed them from their human shape and made them one again with all surrounding mysteries, with the wind and weather, the wilderness and the beasts therein. Her desires now crept out of their little cradles like terrible wolfhounds. She longed to be one of the far-famed witches who visited the homesteads with long catskin gloves and hoods drawn over their eyes. With fear and reverence they were brought into the house and richly entertained, with a roasted snake's heart as the chief dainty. She knew that. To frighten men and women, to be shunned for her malice and to hear the sound of weeping, was what she longed for. Light as a little bird with downy feathers and broad wings, she would fly before the storm along wooded ridges and along boundary dikes. In the dead of night she would tear open doors, throw the brooms about, pour water on the embers of the hearth, and wake the sleepers with an unearthly shriek without ever being seen or caught. Little babes she would steal and change about. She would travel many leagues on the holy midwinter's night to lay them by a strange mother or a young maid.

Time after time she tried to speak. Her mouth moved incessantly, now narrow and long, now round and open. But she could recall no sounds but those she had heard as a child about Jorgrimme's mound. She chirped like a cricket or a grasshopper. Distorting her face spasmodically according to the different sounds, she imitated the cry of the nightjar. Finally she clasped her hands around the neck of her son and with upturned face hissed out a piercing shriek. As he looked at her he was irresistibly compelled to join in the same persistent shriek—and it resounded through the woods.

The blood rushed to his eyes so that he seemed to stare at her through a red film. Then all clear consciousness vanished for a long time and he did not know how he came back into the open and found the way home. Many times she uttered the same shrill cry, and each time he joined in with wild force, but already she was far away. Her cry came from the ford, where all paths ceased and the wilderness began. His temples throbbed and were cold as ice. And he was surprised to find himself carrying something in his arms which was round and smooth to the touch but not heavy.

Only when he felt wet about the feet, and the boughs no longer pricked and scratched him, was he aware that he was once more walking through long meadow grass. He recognized the dark gable of Folketuna when at last it rose before him in the dusk and barred his way.

The thralls were back already and snoring on the floor. Behind the partition Tova lay sighing among the goats and sheep. Without relinquishing the horn, he threw himself upon the straw in the first empty place he could find. He thought his mother was sitting on his chest uttering her long-drawn shriek, but that he could no longer join in it because her elbow was on his throat.

"You're moaning in your sleep," said Tova. "Turn over on the other side."

"Yes," he answered. "I found an old drinking-horn in the forest and it brings me bad dreams."

Towards morning Folke Filbyter came home. He was still wearing Ulf Ulfsson's cloak, but it now bore many stains of mead and beer. He called to Tova to get up at once and light the fire.

VI

FOLKE FILBYTER took his best harness into the yard to be cleaned, as he and his son were to ride to Ulf Ulfsson's on an errand of betrothal. While the thralls were busy with this, they began to cry out and point towards the woods. Before anyone knew what was the matter, they had flocked about the door.

A dark crowd of queer-looking human creatures approached through the oaks. Finn dwarfs they could not be, they were too big for that. Nor did they belong to Ulf Ulfsson's people, for they did not wear the thralls' grey homespun, but cloaks and jerkins of every possible colour and material. And among their rags gleamed the most splendid clasps and buckles. Their faces were unwashed and dark as grained oak, and the men's were bearded up to the eyes. Some of the women wore kerchiefs that had once been white and showed that they were renegade priestesses who had deserted their altars and holy walls. At their head walked a man who was taller than the rest, and on his shoulder he carried a club such as the peasants used for driving stakes into the ground. He raised his right hand as a sign that he was a friend and had no design of attacking.

"Have your folk gone blind, Folke Filbyter," he said, "that they do not know their old friends? We have met often enough by the swamp and helped each other with troublesome wayfarers. Have you grown afraid of Elk the Club King and his robber band? Or has your new friendship with the noble Ulf Ulfsson made you so proud that you will no longer be seen with such rude vagabonds? Speak out, that I may know."

Fear was a thing that had never found a place in Folke Filbyter's soul. On seeing what sort of people he had to deal with, he ordered his thralls to go back to their work at once. And then Elk the Club King and all his followers began to salute him with marks of the deepest reverence and their eyes showed undisguised admiration and attachment. It was the first time the master of Folketuna had been greeted with so much respect.

"In one thing we are equals, we two," Elk went on, bowing more humbly than ever. "You and I have both committed crimes beyond atonement. You have attacked men bathing and sleeping. You are as great a miscreant as I, and yet you manage to live on your estate like a rich landowner, and, compared with you, I am only a bungler at the game. For that reason we all have a sincere admiration for you. We have always treated you as one of ourselves and have never taken so much as a sheep from you. It has been hard enough at times, for we have to suffer cold and hunger, but we will offer you no harm."

The thralls laughed scornfully, and Folke Filbyter dropped his eyes.

"All that is very well," he answered, with rather more haste than was usual with him; "but what would you with me now?"

"I will offer you friendship and fellowship. I know all about what is going on here. I know you mean to visit Ulf Ulfsson to buy a bride. If that visit turns out amiss, there will be discord between you and that worthy man, as there has always been between me and him. He and I are not of the same breed. But then I will help you to plunder him on the roads. He is poor beside you and short of men, but if one day you need help, I can come and guard your house."

"And what do you ask for this service?"

"One thing only. But to me it will be a great honour and as great an insult to Ulf Ulfsson when you go a-courting for your son under his proud roof. The only condition I make is that you swear blood-brotherhood with me on the spot."

The veins in Folke Filbyter's bull neck swelled. But when he heard the laughter of his housecarls and bethought him how gladly he would challenge his neighbour while seeking to win him over, a blind defiance rose within him. He felt rich enough to disregard the law-abiding franklins who stood by the hour wrangling at the Thing instead of striking a blow.

"Master, you will not put fresh disgrace upon the house?" said the bailiff. "Let us fetch our axes and defend the door."

It was unwisely spoken, for instead of an answer Folke Filbyter bared his arm. Elk the Club King instantly did the same and advanced towards him.

The thralls turned away in disgust and skulked back to the saddles, but could not help turning round from curiosity.

They saw the robber draw his knife and cut a piece of turf from the ground. Then he made a pretty deep gash in Folke Filbyter's outstretched arm and another in his own. When the blood of both had mingled in the hole, he replaced the turf so that the roots of the grass stood in the blood.

"Grow, grow, green grass, as grows our friendship!" he said. "Folke Filbyter, you are now foster-brother to the man of worst repute in the whole country-side."

With that he clasped Folke's hand and bowed as deeply as before, his eyes gleaming with devoted admiration.

"Robber," said Folke Filbyter as he led him into the house to drink with him, "I have never before sworn blood-brotherhood with any man."

"And I have reached the height of my ambition," replied Elk. "I ask nothing of you. You gave me more than enough when you mingled your blood with mine. But go now to Ulf Ulfsson, and call upon me when there is need."

When he came out again and went off with his band, the thralls led out two horses and saddled them.

"What shall we all come to?" they whispered.

Folke Filbyter then took his son with him and rode to Ulf Ulfsson's house.

There Ingevald saw things he knew only from the tales of the thralls, and he was silent and abashed even before dismounting. The last part of the road was more even than the floor of the hall at Folketuna. In the grove which lay beside it stood a grave-mound with sacrificial altars, and he counted as many as five runic stones erected to the memory of fallen fathers and brothers. His footsteps were scarcely heard as he entered the hall, so deeply was it strewed with sprigs of juniper and fresh wild flowers. The walls were covered with blue hangings, on which fully armed vikings sailed in their ships or ran their spears through gaping dragons. The table was spread with a white cloth, and round loaves lay beside each wooden platter. Upon the posts of the high seat gleamed weapons of ancient dwarfs' work, and in the sunlight which streamed down upon the hearth even the kettles shone brightly among the black cinders. The thralls, who were seated in a ring making baskets, at once rose courteously on seeing the strangers, and none of them carried a whip at his belt. Before the women's bench at the end of the hall stood Ulf Ulfsson's eldest daughter measuring out thread, and she spoke freely and cheerfully to her maids as though to equals. When one of them dropped the ball of thread, she stooped down and picked it up herself.

Ingevald had never believed such magnificence existed except in the waking dreams of some thrall who lay in the straw making up stories. He felt stiff and awkward in the new blue clothes that had been given him that morning, and he kept behind his father. Step by step he followed him, trying in every way to behave like him. But when Folke Filbyter spread himself on the guest bench and made his voice echo through the room, Ingevald found it unwise to imitate him in everything. He squeezed in beside him and obstinately clung to his narrow seat, not daring to move or even to look up; and he felt so ashamed of him that he would have blushed, had he been capable of it. Puny and silent he sat on the soft cushion, wishing himself at home among the thralls at Folketuna.

But nothing in the whole hall inspired him with such dread and respect as Ulf Ulfsson himself. He sat in the high seat shafting arrows. But as soon as he saw his guest, he went to meet them and signed to his daughter Holmdis and to his two sons. Except in age they were both very like him, and by the firm grasp of their hands Ingevald felt that he was greeting young chiefs who were used to action and command. Holmdis came forward with the mead-horn, and when the guests had been welcomed Ulf Ulfsson seated himself again in the high seat and told stories of bygone heroes. Now and then he took down his harp from the post and played.

He had a younger daughter whose name was Ulfva, but she sat by herself on the women's bench and played.

From time to time Holmdis came back with a fresh horn, and each time it was bigger and handsomer than the last, but

Ingevald knew neither how he ought to receive it nor how much it was becoming to drink. He no longer depended on his father's example, but tried to behave like Holmdis's brothers, though he found it a difficult art. She spoke to him several times frankly and brightly, but his tongue seemed tied so that he could answer nothing. Once she came so near to him that her hair swept across his hands and gleamed in a beam of sunlight. She smiled and turned round.

"Beware of my hair," she said; "it is strong enough to make a bow-string."

A slight frown darted across her candid face like an echo of her last words. Then for the first time it became clear to him that it was she who was destined to live with him at Folketuna. Such boundless happiness seemed to him beyond belief and idle to desire, and he grew more afraid of her than ever. He looked up at the opening in the roof, and she, not knowing he did so from embarrassment, said:

"You are listening for something."

"What is that murmur in the air?" he asked, relieved to find something to say at last.

"Don't you know that either?" she said. "That is the great lime-tree, our guardian tree. It is so old and year by year it spreads farther over the house. The first of the Ulfungs' race planted it long, long ago, and the spirit who dwells in the lofty stem watches over us all from birth. So we too watch over her and her tree. Come out and I will show you round the place."

He took hold of the edge of the table to get up from his cramped seat on the bench. Folke Filbyter pointed with his head at the two young people as they went out, but Ulf Ulfsson continued to play on his harp.

The sun was shining gloriously. Such brightness flashed from her hair and from the clasp on her breast as though the whole flood of sunlight had settled about her and followed her everywhere. Her shadow crept along, racing each step and vanishing under her feet. All the flowers in the grass were opened wide, and the foliage, penetrated by the sun's fires, showed a brighter green than usual. In every spring and every brook lay a sun; even the little puddles on the rocks had their suns great and small, and all in rivalry threw back their beams towards their shining mother in the firmament.

"To-day Odin and Frigga are sitting in their tower Hlidskjalf, looking out over the world," said Holmdis. "What can it be that so delights the holy pair that they shed such glorious radiance upon all creation at this moment?"

She pointed up at the murmuring tree and showed Ingevald that it would take three or four men with outstretched arms to reach around the stem. And she told him how at the feast of Yule she and her women adorned the boughs with eggshells and cocks' feathers to delight the guardian spirit and thank her for a good year. Then she hurried on before him, since she knew the way. He was not surprised at her joyousness, as she walked in such a splendour of light, but he was ashamed at having nothing to say.

"I have been told that you are quick at answers," she said, and asked him which flowers were the fairest, the white or the blue.

To this he could find no answer. Only when they reached the stables and cattle-sheds did he feel more at home.

"This ox's hoofs are too long, he will never be a good draught animal," he began, and his voice at once became more confident. "And never ride that horse; he has a vicious eye. Horses are strange creatures and it is not easy to make them out. Taming horses is like taming women, Father says."

"It is well that one can't judge by the horsehair," she replied with a rapid glance at his head. "I was so curious to see you, Ingevald. I was so sure you would have on the long jerkin of gaudy rags that Father talked about when he came back from Folketuna. And now all I have seen is the big silver rings in your ears. Is it true, as the thralls tell us, that you kneel over a spring in the woods to look at your image?"

He felt that her gaiety was not quite so free from malice as he had thought at first, and that she was making fun of him. He was still standing in the stall examining the horse's eye.

"Now I know the answer to your question about the flowers!" he suddenly exclaimed, turning round. "The white are the fairest, because the bog myrtle's flower is white, and cool bog-myrtle beer on a hot day is the best thing there is, says Father."

"No, the blue are, for of them the bridal wreath is made," she answered as curtly. "And now we must not stand here any longer, but go back into the sunshine."

"He who places the bridal wreath on your brow, Holmdis, will be too dazed to see the colour of the flowers," he said.

He tried to meet her eyes firmly, pleased with the answer he had made. She had pushed the door open and walked out ahead of him.

"He who places the bridal wreath on my brow! Ah, Inge-vald, perhaps I played with him as a child. But now I dare not think of it. Perhaps I have not yet met him, but I have heard my brothers speak of many noble and high-minded warriors. When the proudest and most famous of them rides in at my father's gate, we may begin to talk of my bridal wreath."

"A haughty maid has long to wait."

"And while she is waiting, she spins merrily and sings of her warrior steering his bark far out at sea. Ah, she can hear so plainly how he too sings of her, though perhaps he knows not where she lives nor what is her name."

"And then she falls a-weeping . . . and takes the heir to her neighbour's lands."

She stooped down and plucked a downy dandelion and blew on it.

"No, to her neighbour's son she will say: 'Beware, boy, of my hair, for though it is not horsehair it is strong enough to make a bow-string.'"

He stopped abruptly and tried to find a hateful word to throw at her like a cold stone knife, but she stood up and said calmly: "It is wrong of me to keep you out here so long, when Father is playing the harp. You might have more pleasure in listening to him, for I am sure you have no harp at Folketuna. Now we have talked together and I think it best that we go back to the others."

As they reached the door of the hall, Folke Filbyter interrupted his host's playing and cried:

"You give us too much of your harping, Ulf Ulfsson!

The young people are back already, and our parley has not yet begun! It is not the custom that they themselves should be present and thus hinder our speaking freely in so serious a discussion."

Ulf Ulfsson hung up his harp on the post of the high seat. As a sign that the betrothal was now under debate, all sat with their feet crossed and their hands crossed before them on the table.

"It is true that the young people themselves are not usually present," he said, and his voice was not so clear and firm as before. "But I give them leave to be here, that we may hear what they think. Let them sit in their rightful places, so that I have my daughter beside me and you your son. Now let us hear your business, neighbour. I ask you first, according to old custom: Will you buy land?"

Folke Filbyter stood up. "No."

"Then I ask you: Will you buy grain?"

"No, I will buy one of your daughters, Ulf Ulfsson, and the elder for choice. I do not ask who was her mother, for she is dead. Your daughter's fair form speaks best of her value."

"That is well said," answered Ulf's sons. They showed their agreement by bringing down the right hand upon the left, which still lay on the table before them.

"So far, then, we are agreed. I ask you in like manner to put no questions about Ingevald's mother, for she has fled to the woods again and may therefore also be counted dead. Like for like."

Ulf's sons muttered something about the "Finn woman," but Folke Filbyter hurried on with his speech, which he had learnt by heart.

"It may surprise you that I am all at once so zealous in a matter which a few days ago had not entered my thoughts. In that case you are yourself to blame, Ulf Ulfsson. You came to me. You spoke in many ways as a wise neighbour, but at the same time so offensively that I see only one means of atonement. And that is a marriage bargain between our children."

Ulf Ulfsson nodded thoughtfully.

"If it offended you to hear the truth, Folke Filbyter, then

let me tell you that there are more ways than one of settling
the matter. If you think we have both stayed too long at
home to wield a sword, then we have sons who are young
enough for single combat. Nevertheless I shall not forget that
as a guest you are to-day under my special protection and
that it was myself who first spoke of a marriage. Nay, I
set such store by prudence and calmness that for my part I
will take back my hasty words and at least I will not set my
face against your proposal. The sight of you and your son
and your Folketuna filled me with wrath. You must forgive
it if you will be as prudent as I. But at the same time I
must remind you that at the betrothal everyone is free to speak
his mind without offence to others. And now I turn to you,
my sons. Bethink you that I am growing old and that I shall
be left alone here when you are out with your ships. I need
one who will help me to guard my house and lands. Soon
it will be hard to say who is lord over Svea's land. The
Valkyries' steeds are neighing loudly for a field of blood."

Holmdis sprang up from the cushion beside him. And now
all the sunshine had vanished from her face, though once more
she stood in the sunbeam.

"Father," she said, "do not give me to that man. Never
will I follow him of my free will, though he fill your shield
with gold. And to you, my good brothers, do I turn for help!"

Folke Filbyter struck the back of the bench angrily with
his fist. As he stood there in his wild strength and health,
with Ulf Ulfsson's stained cloak still clasped over his chest,
he looked like a gigantic savage. His awkward gestures and
his roaring voice seemed to belong to the wild woods and
rocks rather than to the peaceful everyday life of a homestead.
And yet it was impossible not to recognize the rich franklin;
his bloated obesity weighed on him like a burden, his stomach
was more prominent than his chest, so that his jerkin looked
too short in front. He straddled with his feet wide apart
and his flaxen hair hung straight down on either side of his
round, clear-skinned face, beardless as a woman's. The ridicule which persistently clung to him wherever he went, again
surrounded him without his being aware of it.

"Ulf Ulfsson, tame your daughter!" he cried. "Teach
her that a wise settlement is the only foundation of children's

happiness! I am the man to make a more generous bridal bargain than any other. Tell her she shall have two hundred ells of homespun and twenty ells of linen . . . and fifty marks of pure silver with the stamp of a Flemish town and . . ."

Ulf Ulfsson stared in embarrassment at the cinders on the hearth.

"Gently, gently, neighbour," he said. "It is only fair that she should have a word to say, since this question of a bargain is a more tangled one than most. Your son has never been out with a ship and can boast no viking's fame. For these three days I have told her of your riches and of your offer. But it is the way of modest maidens to refuse at first. Perhaps she will listen, more readily to her brothers than to us elders."

Now Holmdis's brothers rose and spoke. The younger gave her a friendly nod and spoke first.

"No one shall force my sister," he said curtly.

Folke Filbyter took a couple of paces forward, as though he would take hold of each as he addressed him.

"You have lost your wits, young men!" he cried. "To each of you, her brothers, I have promised a jerkin with silver buttons, but I am willing to offer more. Do you know what, Ulfungs? You have hangings on your walls and flowers on your floor, but you are poor. Even if your house has the broadest acres, after mine, you are yet poor men!"

The elder brother considered long before he spoke: "I cannot agree with my younger brother. If two young people join together from liking alone, they have not much to build upon. Love is a mead that soon turns sour, but a wise and generous bargain provides interests to be guarded in common. And even if at first their hearts be cool, in time they will find out each other's good sides and rejoice in them and be content. Therefore young people ought never to have a hand in their own marriage, but should leave it to others who see clearly and can arrange all calmly for the best. Dear sister, an old rhyme tells us: Marry for love and find it hollow; but marry wisely and joy shall follow."

Folke Filbyter brightened up and prepared to resume his seat.

"Do you hear that, Holmdis?" he said. "Your elder brother has inherited Ulf Ulfsson's careful prudence."

" 'Twould be well if I had," the elder brother continued; "but I have not yet finished speaking, neighbour. You say truly that we Wolf Cubs are poor by the side of you. Next to yours, our lands are the broadest, but gold and silver do not grow in woods and swamp—except when *you* pass by with a hole in your sack. True, in other summers we brothers have been out a-viking in the West, but there we have had more dealings with iron than with other metals. Thus we have reason to hearken to your offer, but it shall not make us forget the only right answer. And now I turn to you, Ulf Ulfsson, my father and master. Ill does it beseem us, who are of ancient Lawman's stock, to ally ourselves with Folketuna. Gold can do much, but not all. From Folketuna will never come a son who can be our brother in power and repute, and the shining sword of your old age. From a corrupted seed no tree will grow. Can you conceive Folke Filbyter as the ancestor of a mighty lineage? Folketuna is a despised house, founded by a stranger of whom we know nothing but ill. Let him marry his son among thralls or Finn folk. That is fitting for one who, when he dies, will lie forgotten, with no pillar-stone to mark his grave. We believe you meant well, Father, when you made this unhappy proposal; but I tell you frankly that in that hour your wonted prudence had forsaken you. The times are overcast and threatening, but my sister is too good for a bantling of Folketuna. We, her brothers, say 'No' and raise our ban, for we purpose to make our race renowned."

Ulf Ulfsson was the only one who remained seated. He turned and took his daughter by the elbows.

"Now may my good fylgia look into my heart, for my purpose was clean.[8] And you, my daughter, are free-born as I am. For three renowned generations you can count your kindred. Names of heroes famed throughout Svithiod you can read on the stones in the memorial grove. Joyfully you may dream of brothers who fell fighting in foreign lands.

[8] The fylgia was the attendant spirit who watched over every individual.

in going there. He recalled only Holmdis, and he saw her far more clearly now than when he sat before her in the hall. As she measured out the thread for her maids, she brightened all about her, making the work seem a joy. As she walked, she bent her head like a singer, although the words she threw at him were most scornful and meant to turn him away. They had struck him to the heart, so that from that moment he could think of nothing but her. She persecuted and tormented him as he tossed in the straw, imagining that he recalled her brother's long and insulting speech. Illumined by sunbeams, her hair swept across his hands and he felt how strong it was and how glorious it would be to twine it into a bow-string.

"I tell you, Father," he whispered in a quivering voice, "no woman but Holmdis will I ever bring to Folketuna. I shall set her before me on my horse and fetch her by force, because she defied us and because I hate her. I shall tame Ulf Ulfsson's daughter to crawl over the floor for her food."

"That is more boldly spoken than I had looked for from you, Ingevald," his father hastened to answer, as though with a feeling of relief. "Are you sure now that you are speaking the truth and not dissembling your longing for that woman? If you are, I shall not think much of you. I am rich enough to buy you a wife who will think herself lucky to wear the keys of Folketuna."

"You must believe me, Father, I hate her. And why is she called Holmdis? She stood in the sunlight when I saw her first, and Soldis will I call her. "Soldis! Soldis! I will cry all over Folketuna."

Folke Filbyter turned his back on him and swept up more straw for a pillow.

"You are a sorry fellow," he said, once more dull and indifferent. "I can hear well enough how you hate her. You will bring folly to my house, that is what you will do. But do as you will. I had thought of going with you and helping you, but now 'tis all one. Take the bailiff with you and the stoutest of the carls—unless you think better of it and stay where you are. My only advice is to offer a white hen for success at the shrine on your way, though I know nothing more pitiful and contemptible than the gods."

Ingevald jumped up and shook the straw from him. The

bailiff and the younger housecarls had already tied their shoes and stood waiting, though nobody had forbidden them to go to sleep. When he came up to them, they swung their axes in the dusk, for they felt their share in the insult to the house.

To make his revenge the more proud and bitter, he put on his motley dress with the red and yellow patches, though one side of it was torn to pieces. The bailiff kindled a torch in the embers to light him. As they passed Folke Filbyter, they saw that he still lay with his back to the room, not taking the least notice of their proceedings. Each of the thralls had to show that his ax was firmly hafted and that he had a skin wound about his right hand to guard against return blows. This was the equipment they used when out on Folke Filbyter's secret business of plundering wayfarers, and they were as well accustomed to bear arms as to ply the spade. Ingevald therefore did not spend much time on them, being full of impatience and ardour. But for himself he chose a bundle of newly shafted arrows and a bow without a string.

Then he hurried to the stable and mounted the biggest and most powerful of the horses. The thralls flocked about him and followed him on foot with long, dragging steps, carrying their axes on their shoulders.

He stopped at the first shrine beside the way to kill a white hen, as his father had advised. Wild hops and briers climbed about the little round wooden shrine, whose roof was almost hidden under a leafy hazel-bush. As he went in with the blood of the sacrifice, he said: "Tear off a piece of bark from the roof; it is dark in here, though the night is light enough outside. I know it is Freya sitting here with her apple in her hand, but she is always so covered with moss that she looks more like a rotten billet than a goddess. So I am not surprised that to-night her face feels so small and smooth as I smear it with the blood of the offering."

The bailiff tore off a piece of bark so that more light came in, and leaned over the hole to look in.

"Ingevald!" he cried. "This is terrible! What has been done here? Is it the work of men or of wood-spirits? It is a new and strange image whose cheeks you have reddened, and it is a child, not an apple, that the new-comer holds on her knee. Freya was carved from a single block of oak and was much higher."

Ingevald fell back to the entrance and stood there, his hands bloody from the slaughtered hen.

"The worm-eaten remains of Freya have been thrown down," he said, "and over them lies a staff. Come nearer, men! Tell me, have you seen that staff before?"

They raised their axes as though to defend themselves against some invisible thing, drew cautiously nearer, and stopped.

"That is old Jakob's staff!"

"Yes it is his staff," said Ingevald. "I should know it among ten others. All that has to do with that man has burnt itself into my memory, but I remember nothing more plainly than the staff with which I ill-treated him. Now it has betrayed him. How could that pious man do such an evil deed?"

"Ingevald," whispered the bailiff, pulling at his motley jerkin, "Jakob does nothing secretly. You may be sure he left his staff on the broken image that everyone might clearly see who was the culprit. How easily might any of us have been suspected and punished!"

"Well, then," exclaimed Ingevald hotly, turning to the image, "I know you not, goddess, but your face is still young and smooth and shining, and I have taught you to blush. Now I shall make you as fine a crimson as any queen of the South— and you shall help us, if you can!"

So saying, he threw all the remaining blood over the image and snatched his horse from the thralls. Above them the mighty oaks trembled and murmured.

He had blood on his sleeve but did not give himself time to wipe it off. As he rode, he thought of nothing but Soldis and nursed his anger and revenge.

When they came to Ulf Ulfsson's homestead, day was already dawning. No smoke rose from the roof, and all the outhouses were barred. A horse, grazing tethered within the yard, began to neigh, but they felled it with a blow of the ax. Then they struck axes firmly into the wall of the house so that they made a sure stairway, and on them they climbed silently and cautiously up to the roof. When they had crept as far as the smoke-hole, they could see down into the hall and make sure that nobody was awake. A warm smell of burning still rose from the hearth, where earth and ashes had been heaped upon the embers to keep life in them till the morning. They tied three belts together and let themselves down one by one. All came down into the ashes, making them flare up, and they had to help each other to put out the fire which began to smoulder in their clothes and foot-gear. To their relief they had already discovered that the thralls did not sleep with their masters here as at savage Folketuna, but lay by themselves in some separate dormitory. But the doors of the bed stood ajar and they saw Ulf Ulfsson lying asleep within with his sons. Ingevald went forward softly and closed the doors. Then he shot the bolt and placed three thralls with their backs to the doors, to prevent the sleepers opening them from within. The other thralls withdrew the bar from the house-door, so that the way lay open for escape.

All these preparations were carried out cautiously and noiselessly. Only after assuring himself that nobody was stirring in the house did Ingevald begin to search for Soldis. But he had gone only half-way through the hall when he caught sight of her: half awake, bare-footed and with her bare shoulders covered with a brown kerchief, she stood in a doorway staring at him. The big silver rings gleamed in his ears, and all the red and yellow patches fluttered in the air as he ran towards her. She began to call out, first in terror, then in anger. The men in the bed awoke and answered her, but the thralls held the doors fast with their backs. They hammered and tried to prize them open from within, but the bolt was of iron and the thralls' backs were stout, and their feet had got purchase against a piece of timber in the floor.

Ingevald seized her, and as soon as she was bound he took the scissors which lay on the table beside some sewing, cut off her thick yellow hair, and gave it to the bailiff.

"Twine me a bow-string," he said.

The bailiff took some wax from a box on the table and twined a string which he fitted to the bow.

"Open the doors!" said Ingevald.

The thralls drew the bolt and stepped aside so that the doors flew open.

Ulf Ulfsson sat upright in the bed and it was easy to take aim at his grizzled beard, which spread over his chest. The sons lay farther in, so that they could not get out before him, and none of them had any weapon. Ingevald took his longest arrow and laid it to the bow.

The arrow whizzed through the hall, as though a giant lizard of the old dragon brood had shot out its sting. But Ingevald was no good bowman and his arms were shaking with excitement. The arrow only struck Ulf Ulfsson in the hand and nailed it fast to the bedpost, so that he could not free himself.

"There you sit with your sons, Ulf Ulfsson, prudent and deliberate as ever, and can neither get in nor out," Ingevald mocked him. "Do you remember what we were talking of today? To tell the truth, Ulf Ulfsson, I have almost forgotten it. And now I take your daughter by force. Soldis she shall be called henceforth. Soldis, Soldis! Tell me now, Soldis, where your father keeps his mead, for I am thirsty and it is fitting to drink at such a marriage."

The sons struggled vainly to free Ulf Ulfsson's hand and to get past him out of their narrow prison.

"Ingevald," whispered the bailiff, "do you not see that our men are throwing down their axes and running out of the door? The noise has roused the people of the house and they are already fighting in the yard. Will you lose your prize and maybe your life for the sake of empty words?"

But Ingevald would not be stopped; hatred and desire clamoured ever more recklessly in his mouth.

"Listen to me, dear Ulf Ulfsson, sitting there so comfortably beside your sons. There is no need of haste, but my thralls are impatient at your tardiness with the ale of welcome. Repeat to me the names of the great heroes of your family. How else shall I answer when your daughter bears me a son and he asks me of the Ulfungs' high lineage? If I know nothing, I can only answer that he shall shaft his first arrow for you, Ulf Ulfsson, and fix it as firmly in your left hand as I have set mine in your right."

The bailiff placed himself before Ingevald so as to cover the bed. Not very imposing did he look in his plain homespun and with his flat face, scored with innumerable little wrinkles. But he was the first to come to his senses, and now he knew his power.

"Every instant may be your last, Ingevald. As yet you are not much more than a thrall at Folketuna, and the thralls are in my charge. Beware of disobeying me. I have my whip here."

These words were enough to awaken the thrall habit in Ingevald and he felt at once that he must obey. The bailiff signed to him to take Soldis by the arms, while he took her feet, and together they ran out of the hall with her. But in the doorway Ingevald turned once more and shouted to the bed:

"You see, dear Father Ulf, how impatient the thralls are to get us into the bridal straw. And your daughter is quite beside herself with longing. I am the only one who keeps his head, and I believe I might have found a more decent mate. She has not even dressed herself. If you were not such a laggard, you might fetch her bridal linen. But sit where you are, since you are so warm and comfortable; think of your children and make rich promises to the gods!"

He lifted the girl and set her before him on the horse. Taking no notice of the flying thralls surrounding him, he dashed forward over stumps and bracken with no thought of fending off the boughs that caught him on the chest and tore the patches from his clothes.

"Soldis, Soldis!" he shouted in triumph, and covered her with wild caresses.

Folke Filbyter stood at his gate as the wild band rushed into the yard. He saw the bloodstains on his son's sleeve and asked: "How many corpses lie on the bench in Ulf Ulfsson's hall?"

Ingevald reined in his sweating horse without at first being able to collect his thoughts. Then he remembered it was the blood of the sacrificed hen, and, panting, he related all that had happened.

" 'Twould have been a manlier shot if the bow-string had not been a fair woman's hair," his father answered.

Ingevald lifted Soldis down from the horse. Meanwhile he continued to tell of his offering at the shrine and of old Jakob's staff.

"I hear the old man goes about preaching of a goddess he

calls Jesu Mother. I believe the new image was hers. It was Jesu Mother who guided the arrow so that Ulf Ulfsson could neither slay nor be slain."

Folke Filbyter answered him contemptuously: "If it is as you say, then Jakob is bolder than I thought. I have often had a mind to do what he has done and break the wretched images to pieces. But they stand on my ground and here no one is master but I. Let us none the less be prudent, even if we have not the lofty wisdom of the Ulfungs. Take up his staff from Freya's image and set it above the stable-door. Who knows?—perhaps it will guard us against fire and thieves. And now go you indoors, Ingevald. In the corner opposite the sheep-fold I have made ready a place apart for you and the woman, with posts and skins. It looks like a grey tent of the Finn folk, and you will be warm there in winter. And I have put a new lock on the house-door, so that you can fasten it from outside until you have broken her to subjection."

He did not bestow a glance on Soldis, but left his son to carry her in alone. Then he went back to the gate and carefully counted the thralls who had returned from the nocturnal raid, to make sure that none was missing. Some of them had blood on their faces, and he washed their wounds himself and bandaged them with earth. He also examined all the holes in their clothes and showed how to mend them. The bailiff was highly praised for his ready assumption of command, and when all was in order Folke Filbyter offered his weary housecarls a sumptuous breakfast with much beer.

"Perhaps it is best as it is," he said, "though I would rather have seen Ulf Ulfsson a corpse. But after this we may expect much trouble. Ulf Ulfsson is not so simple a man as to go to the Thing and raise a suit against me. If I have not had time to ride to the Thing before, I shall have still less hereafter. We have to consider that his sons are brave men and proud, but he has not many men about the place and his thralls are little used to handling weapons. Therefore they will want time to prepare and we can fortify ourselves. Those of you who have skill in the smith's craft must quickly make a fire in the forge. The rest of you are to take out the horses and all our wagons and sledges, though it is summer, and fetch stones from the forest. We have no rocky

height in the neighbourhood, but close to the fields lies the
knoll the herdsmen call Bellerbo, because they have made a
pen there for the goats. It has a good spring too, known
for its clear water and its friendly water-sprite. There we
will make haste to build a ring-work of stones and tree-trunks,
so that we may have a refuge if it should go so badly with
us that we cannot defend the house against attack. I had
thought to sit here in peace with my ploughs and spades, but
the storm-clouds have risen faster than I could have dreamt
a few days ago. Now there is no turning back, and if I
meet Ulf Ulfsson I shall kill him."

Refreshed by their hearty meal and pleased at his eager-
ness to defend the honour of the house, they all hastened to
obey his orders. All day long they worked at Folketuna, and
the sledges grated over the heather as they drew the heavy
stones. Soot and sparks shot out of the turf roof of the
forge, and Folke Filbyter himself sat on the blackened block
by the side of the anvil. His old coat of mail was unrolled
and cleaned of rust, and he had made for himself a helmet
of a peculiar kind. He fetched out one of the ordinary small
round helmets that lay in the armoury and had a brim fitted
to it. Only once in his life had he seen an iron hat of this
sort on the head of a warrior, at the storming of a town in
the Danelagh, and he had noticed that it gave good protection
against all kinds of missiles, whether arrows or stones. The
smiths found it ugly and heavy and were unwilling to rivet
it together, but he forced them to go on with it.

Tired after a sleepless night and all the unwonted bustle
of the day, he gradually dropped his chin on his breast and
fell asleep as he sat on the block. In his dreams he still saw
the smiths turning the helmet on the anvil and hammering
in the rivets.

He dreamed he was sitting in the workshops of the underworld, where the sooty beings of Muspelheim ran about with
red-hot forgings without feeling the sparks that settled on
their crooked, hairy legs. They ground their teeth and thrust
out the glowing iron towards the door, as though expecting
a visit from those they most hated and feared. Outside there
was a sound of tramping and the dragging of spears in the
sand. It could be none other than the Æsir, of whom Jor-

grimme had spoken and who were still engaged in their search. But Freya came into the shower of sparks, tall and buxom, with her broad open teeth looking like bits of apple set in her lips. "They search and search and see nothing," she whispered, hanging over his shoulder so that the jewels on her breast jingled and swayed. "The seed they search for, I have now hidden in the fertile and life-giving soil."

He reeled under the weight of the beautiful goddess and clutched her arm. But never had he felt an arm so sleek and smooth and yet so iron-hard. Just as he had hold of it, the fire blazed up in the forge and woke him with its glare.

"Is that how you mind your work?" he said to the smiths. "If I doze off for a moment in a senseless dream, you stop at once. The helmet is far from finished, and evening will soon be here."

"Aye, but you stretched out your hand over the anvil," answered the smiths, leaning on their hammers. "Would you have us strike it?"

VII

DURING the time which followed, Soldis was seldom seen outside the house. No one ever heard her speak a friendly word either to masters or thralls. At the slightest sound at night, she stood upright and listened. Sometimes she would stand thus till morning, whiter than a lily and motionless as a Valkyrie in a wall-hanging. She always listened in the direction of the woods, for she expected to hear her brother's horses from that quarter.

Ingevald kept watch over her, sitting within the tent of skins. He could not face the thralls for shame at not having tamed her. Whenever anyone was listening, he pretended to be stern and commanding and began to threaten and insult her. Or else he made as though all was well between them and flattered her with fair words. But when the others were asleep, he crept up to her and begged for love and kissed her kirtle and bowed down before her in the straw, as though asking her to tread upon him. And yet in the midst of his sorrow he was filled with a dizzy joy which danced and sang in his poor restless heart. He lived in a whirl of delight and despair. Love tore away the curtain from life, so that life was brought closer to him, so close that he reflected it like a sheet of water. Things which before had been indifferent or clear as day were changed to problems. He began to brood on life and death and good and evil. The eternal murmur of the World-Tree, which is heard only by brooders or lovers, fanned his thoughts and raised them on high like eagles or doves. There was no great and noble deed that he would not perform, simply because it now had acquired a charm previously unknown. He dreamed of the lofty beauty of the Æsir and of Jesu Mother. Their radiant forms possessed his mind so that he was scarcely able to speak of trifling everyday things. His remorse for the outrage was drowned in a feeling that it was a proud and daring deed. Although he sat all night without closing his eyes and watched

Soldis as she stood listening, he was blind to the bitter reality and believed he sat thus only to admire her and enjoy his happy thoughts. In the morning, when Tova began sighing in the sheep-fold and the thralls assembled to rake the embers from the ashes, he rose hurriedly.

"Soldis, Soldis!" he would then say. "Delling's dwarf is singing from Breidablik his greeting to the world at dawn.[9] Well must you have slept if you are already awake. Shall I take you to the spring that you may wash and sit in the grass wreathing garlands? Or shall I lead you to the paddock, where thirty horses stand with their heads on each other's necks? There I will lift you on to the bough of an oak and make sport for you with the colts. They are not so easy to catch, for they keep with their dams in the midst of the herd. But why do you listen to the forest rather than to me, Soldis? Do you not know that your brothers have few horses and few men? Long will it be ere they can arm. And if they do, Folketuna will then possess a stronghold with a gate of iron which will defy both fire and sword. And never shall you go from me alive."

She never made him any answer, but when it was full daylight she went into the tent and lay down and slept.

In this way the whole long winter went by, when often in the morning the floor about the hearth was white with snow that had fallen through the smoke-vent. Now and then he would take her out in the sledge, but he always had a sword with him under the wolfskins. And as soon as they came where the forest was thick, he turned and drove home.

One day her little sister Ulfva came walking through the woods by herself. The cold had pinched her cheeks and made them look like red and white flowers. Nobody could understand how she had found her way so far, but the men had not the heart to do her any harm and brought her into the hall. On seeing Soldis, she began to dance and ran and threw herself into her arms, but Ingevald guessed she was the bearer of some message, and kept close to them.

"I can see full well that you are sad, Sister," Ulfva whispered; "but how glad I am to see you again!"

---

[9] Delling ("bright") was the father of the Day. It was the dwarf Thjodreyrir who sang strength to the gods (Æsir), as recited by Odin in the *Hávamál.*—Breidablik ("broad view") was Balder's dwelling.

Soldis thought how she might frame her words warily and find out something, and at last she asked:

"Our brothers must have got many new horses since I was at home?"

"No, no, Sister; our brothers have no new horses," the child answered.

"Then Father must have bought many new thralls?"

"No, he has bought no thralls. He has only the old ones, and they are getting older and older every day. Don't you remember Snug, how old and lame he was? He can scarcely walk now. It is the winter cold that he can't stand. And Onne, good, faithful Onne, has hurt his hand badly. He cut himself with the ax when he was splitting wood. Sharp is still the best worker. Father has such old thralls, but then they have always been with us and he gets on best with them, he says."

Soldis was irresolute.

"You have grown, Ulfva, it is a joy to see you growing into a little lady. But tell me, was it Father who sent you here?"

"Father did not know I was going."

"Child, have you walked this long and dangerous way without Father's leave?"

"Yes, Father was out hunting."

"So Father knew nothing of it."

Ingevald laughed.

"No, Father knew nothing," he interjected; "but your brothers, your brothers?"

The child was frightened and stepped back.

"Why do you both speak so harshly to me, when I only came to see you, sister?"

He seized her roughly by the elbows and shook her.

"Speak the truth at once, it was your brothers who sent you!"

She began to cry and he had to let her go again.

"I mustn't say anything," she sobbed, cringing against the wall.

"Now understand me, Ulfva," said Soldis. "It is better that you betray all to us both, so that at least I may know something, than that you keep it from me. You see that we cannot talk together unheard. . . . Are my brothers never coming to fetch me?"

"Fetch you?"

"Yes; what did my brothers say to each other on the night when I was carried off?"

"I was asleep, Sister. I never knew you were carried off against your will. Nobody has ever told me that. I thought it was a custom that a bride should ride away at night with torches and attendants."

Soldis paled and kissed the child's forehead.

"Then am I quite forgotten in my father's house?"

"No, no, Sister. Father and our brothers speak of nothing but you as they sit by the fire at work. They say they have nothing in the world but you. And they have taken out your old clothes and laid them in the chest that stands in the pantry. I have seen more than one of them steal in there, too, when he thought nobody was looking. And I have tried to follow, but the door has always been bolted on the inside."

"And it was my brothers who sent you here?"

"They wanted me to see how you fared. They knew that nobody would harm me. For safety's sake they took from me everything that was of silver."

"And was there nothing you were to say to me, Ulfva?"

"Yes; three words I was to say to you: 'Patience, patience, patience!'"

Soldis stiffened and drew herself up, turning yet paler. Her eyes looked over the child's head without seeing her.

"Take my brothers the kiss I gave you," she said, and then her voice grew hard. "Tell them I am a happy udalwoman at rich Folketuna, married to a noble and famous franklin's son."

Ingevald's excited state of mind, swaying continually between tenderness and tyranny, lent him a fine ear. He understood well enough the defiant scorn of her answer, but noticed at the same time the despairing helplessness which her words were intended to conceal—or to reveal, as one might take them. He felt that this time the defiance was not addressed to him alone, but also to her brothers. He was enraptured by what she had said, and repeated it twice over to the little one, that she might forget nothing. Then he took her by the hand and led her out of the house, still crying, but silently. She looked around in confusion, but no longer dared to think of running back to embrace her stern sister once again.

As he came out, he ordered two of the housecarls to take their axes and accompany him to the wood. They had not gone far when they caught sight of two of the Ulfssons' thralls who stood waiting, also armed with axes. Then he let the girl go and charged her once more not to forget Soldis's answer. After that he returned home with his attendants without approaching the armed men from the enemy's house.

He wondered greatly what the sons of Ulf had meant by the thrice repeated message: patience. He often thought of it later and at times it reassured him, but more often it filled him with an indefinite and growing uneasiness.

He saw that from that hour Soldis began to fade away and nevermore rose up at night to listen. To try her, he sometimes went out in the middle of the night, leaving the house-door open. As long as he could bear the cold, he hid behind the corner of the stable, but she never even rose and went to the door. When he came back, he found her sleeping heavily and unconcerned. On other nights, when he heard she was awake, he pretended to be asleep in order the better to spy on her. With the skins drawn up to his eyes, he lay watching the moonlight quivering with frost, or else he made the time go by trying to distinguish the thralls by the difference in their snoring. But still she lay quietly in her place with her back turned towards him, seeming no longer to think of flight or rescue.

Little by little the winter drew towards its end and signs of summer appeared in fields and meadows. Happy and yet a stranger he sat beside her, when at last she bore him a son.

Old Tova, who was the midwife of the place, carried the child out into the yard to Folke Filbyter. He was sitting on a stone, resting after his work. She laid the boy stark naked on the yellow flowers at his feet.

"Soldis has now borne us this man child," she said, "It is for you, master, to decide whether I am to expose it in the wastes or give it back to its mother. If you will hearken to us thralls, we say, let it live. May a good fylgia take care of the little one. Not many children have been born in your house. The Finn woman has taken to the woods, and for many a long year you have had no news of your elder sons. Long ago I used to hear them whispering together, and I know they never felt at ease here. Youth longs for adventure and exploits.

Maybe they have such love for their ship and the open sea that they will never come back. Perhaps, like many other vikings, they have seized lands and a stronghold on other shores. Perhaps they have already fallen."

Her heart was beating violently as she tried to give her drawling speech as fine and persuasive a tone as possible. And her anxiety increased when her master did not answer at once but seemed lost in thought.

"Much evil is spoken of Folketuna," she muttered, feeling her way; "but we thralls know that at heart you are a good master."

He looked up.

"Why were not my sons as contented as I? Can a couple of upright timbers bring honour to a house simply because they are called high-seat posts? Why must everything here be the same as in other places? Why must we all be alike? May not a man live as he pleases? Do I sleep worse in my straw than Ulf Ulfsson in his closed bed? No, no, wild Folketuna shall remain as it is. Every bush cannot bear the mawkish hip. Much evil is spoken about us, and many slain wayfarers lie in the swamp. I regret nothing, you miserable gods, but with this child you strike fear into me."

Tova signed to the other thralls that they should come and aid her prayers. They left their tools and came slowly, one by one, until there was a ring about him. They felt that, of all that till then had happened at Folketuna, this moment was the most fateful. For the houses and the holy fields and they themselves would all pass one day to this new-born creature, if it were granted life as a bounty.

When she saw the whole crowd assembled, she took heart and remembered her duty as midwife.

"It is the custom," she said, though at first her voice still quivered a little, "that the midwife shall entreat for the child. Therefore you must have patience with me, master, and not take it ill. We thralls have not yet forgotten the shameful reproaches which we once heard from the mouth of Ulf Ulfsson. Now a child has been born that has your blood and his. And would you refuse it life simply because he is your worst enemy? Let the boy grow up and one day guide the great plough. Let him then ride to the thing-stead and take his place by the greatest stone in the judgment-circle. It shall be known as Folketuna's doom-stone, and from it he shall speak for us before the other udalmen, so that honour and repute shall be ours. Command me rather to pluck out your own eye, master, than to bear away the boy."

She felt already that the victory was half won as she heard the loud approval of the other thralls around her. She thought her master brightened and was more of her mind than he yet cared to show. All the time he looked down at the child, and after considering awhile longer he said:

"In former days I was feared and secure and might have passed calmly into the sleep of death, but now it seems the Ulfssons have forgotten neither the rape nor the wounding. One day they will come, and, if they can, they will take away the child. How have misfortune and feud grown up from nothing in less than a year! I have nothing to trust to but my own years, which are short and fleeting, and you, thralls. For the first time I need men's help. I have clothed and fed you as myself. My homespun and my food have been your homespun and your food. You have been given sleep and rest, and I have seen that you did not lack your sports and diversions. Can you now keep watch and ward and stand ready with your axes at the gate on the first sound of hoofs?"

"That we promise you by the good Frey! And you can put some trust in the robbers too!" the thralls all cried at once.

Without waiting a moment longer, Tova hastened, as well as her stiff legs were able, to avail herself of this more cheerful mood. She fetched a bowl of water and broke off a twig that was just in leaf and gave them to her master. Then she placed the child on his knees.

He then named the boy by dipping the twig in the water and making the sign of Thor's hammer on his forehead and breast. As a special honour he called him Folke after himself and repeated the name five several times.

"Now lay the child with its mother," he said to Tova. "Meanwhile we others will go and offer a cock at the shrine, since custom demands it and since it is Thor's day."

Ingevald was still sitting in the tent with Soldis and had taken no part in the intercession. But when he saw Tova return with the child, his eyes brightened. If he had been able to flush, his face would have coloured with joy as he thrust his head out of the skin curtains. But the next moment it relapsed into a weary melancholy, as he whispered:

"Soldis has lain in a long, still sleep and she breathes so faintly that I can scarce hear it. Soldis, Soldis, you have not yet forgiven me! Why will you go from me just now?"

Tova laid the child with its mother, but nothing availed to awake her. Then the discreet and experienced bondwoman began to search among all the old lumber at the back of the tent. At last she found the horn that Ingevald had taken from Jorgrimme in his mound. She knew nothing about it, nor did she ask questions; resolutely and with an air of authority, she took the boy in her lap and taught him how to suck from a bull's horn when she had filled it with lukewarm milk and pulled the wooden plug out of the hole in the point. All else was silent in the hall. Healing-herbs were boiling in the pot which hung on chains over the fire; the smoke blew down, making it hard to see, and the swallows flitted to and fro under the roof-tree.

"I fear my herbs will be of no use," she said to Ingevald in a hushed voice. "Go out into the yard and twine the death garland for your beloved!"

By evening Soldis had already ceased to live. All night a mighty fire blazed upon the hearth to guard the house with its licking tongues against powers of evil. Ingevald never moved from her side, and the transports of love still raised his soul so far above earth that his thoughts glittered and sparkled like the starry sky. His loss did not cause him pain, but was felt as a blissful melancholy, and he continued to talk to Soldis, putting to her the closest and most eager questions on life and death, though he never received any answer. Now and then the thralls came and peeped through the curtains to have a sight of her. When they heard his questions, new and strange to them, they said to one another:

"This will be the end of him too. So it is with all the dwarf folk. When once they get a fancy for anything, they cannot stop; and when they begin to brood and ask questions, their soul bursts asunder and dissolves into the air and the wilderness around them."

Next day they cut two logs out of the wall so that they could lift out Soldis without having to take her through the door which belonged to the living. For the first time she wore a wreath and a bridal head-dress, and she was set upon the back of the same horse that Ingevald had ridden when he brought her to the house. He held one of her hands and the bailiff the other, and in this way they led the silent rider to an open space in the oak-forest, immediately before the shrine of Jesu Mother. Dry wood had already been stacked in a narrow ring with an entrance on one side. They forced the horse backwards into the ring and then closed the entrance with wood as high as the bridle. When that was done, the bailiff struck the horse a blow of the hammer on his forehead so that he sank on his knees, but the wood all round held up the slaughtered animal and kept him from falling. Thus Soldis still sat upright in the saddle. Ingevald reached over the pile, still holding her hand as firmly as though he would never let her go. And all the while he continued his questions.

"Are you to the very last so proud and hard that you will not answer me? What do you see now? High as you sit, you must see far, though there be never so great a crowd around you of old men and women and children who flock continually about Hel's gate. Soldis, you come on horseback like a Valkyrie! Has the key already been turned? Does the darkness hide all things from you, that you have nothing to answer? Is it the whistling of the Heiptas' thorny scourges that terrifies you? [10] Naught have you to fear, Soldis. Take your seat calmly on the bench at Urd's Thing-stead and await your judges. [11] And if you have no spoken runes to guard you, I have to-night taught your good fylgia all she is to say. Or do you already walk upon the path of joy among the honeyed flowers, letting my questions speed past like little black flies that no one cares to catch? If you would but answer me once in the faintest whisper, I should know something. Now I must myself answer all my questions, and you cannot guess what my answers will be. The image of Jesu Mother is not more silent beneath its roof of bark than you on your motionless charger. Come hither, thralls, and help me in my questioning! And come out, master and Father, and

[10] Hel is properly the name of the goddess of the dead. The Scandinavian Hell was the abode of all those who died a natural or "straw" death; not necessarily a place of torment.—The Heiptas were tormenting spirits who punished evil-doers after death.

[11] Urd was the first of the Norns. Her province was the past; her sisters dealt with the present and future.

mock at the gods you despise! For they have plundered your house."

The thralls would not listen to him, and at last they persuaded him to let go her hand and fling the torch upon the pile. A vat of consecrated mead was borne out upon the grass, and the more they drank, the wilder was their sorrow. The women shook out their hair and wailed in long quavering lamentations. Tova ran up to the fire itself and threw two dice to the dead woman.

"The time may be long for you, mistress!" she cried. "With these dice you may shorten many a gloomy hour. They are carved from the precious tooth of the elephant, mistress, and they are all that is left to me from my young days."

Then the others began running into the flames with different gifts, and their sorrow changed to anger.

"Here are needle and thread and wax for you!" they cried one after the other, shaking the dead woman by the arm to make her hear them. "How else could you help yourself when your clothes need mending? Your nails are cut and we have carefully washed you and combed your hair. Here are high boots to protect you from the thorns in the dark valley. Here is a pan to cook your food and a lighted lamp to show you the way. Let your judges see them, that they may know we have honoured you as a legally bought udalwoman, though you were scarcely more than a captive. And ask them, ask them from us thralls, whether they have forgotten the oath of Valland! Ask them whether they heard the oath of the son of Ivalde, that when he had destroyed their golden halls and themselves, there should be no more thralls on earth!"

Fired by the mead and the general turmoil, where none could distinguish between mourning and lust of vengeance, Ingevald at last plucked the great silver rings from his ears and forced his way in under the flames.

"Here is fine silver for you, Wife!" he cried. "The Finn woman's heritage. Hold it out to the ice-bearded ones in the judgment-seat. Tell them that Mimer too was present when the dwarfs were made from the limbs of Ymer. Hang the rings in Freya's ears and tell her that when I rode out to fetch you, I sacrificed to Jesu Mother. It was she who saved your father's life. It was Jesu Mother who rescued me from being his slayer."

The smoke from the pile that consumed Ulf Ulfsson's best-loved daughter rolled its heavy clouds over the homestead and into the hall, where Folke Filbyter sat entirely alone with the child, not caring to show Soldis any marks of honour. But he had given orders not to stint the mead. So it was a long time before the funeral-ale was finished and the ashes put into the earth.

At last a reeling, staggering crowd appeared in the doorway and their shouts of laughter echoed through the house. Their eyes and cheeks were running with mead, and the thralls embraced and kissed each other, still roaring out their quavering lamentations. But most of them were trying to invent the most insulting and obscene recriminations which Soldis was to carry to the Æsir and more especially to the goddesses. They shouted in one another's faces, flung their hands about, caught each other by the waist, and hopped around in a sort of dance.

Ingevald was not to be seen, but the thralls thought it right and natural that Folke Filbyter from henceforth took charge of the child with the same fatherly care with which he had watched over them. For it was his own flesh and blood, and it did not surprise them in the least to see the former sea-king sit rocking the cradle like a woman. But in their heated and drunken state they could not forbear chattering and making merry, and they surrounded him and sank on their knees with shouts of laughter when they saw how clumsy he was at his new task. Fearing the Ulfssons might choose that day for an attack, he had donned his byrnie and wore a short sax-sword at his side. On the bench beside him lay the huge iron hat, which was still bright as silver round the rivets.

The women thought he would frighten the child when he leaned over the bag of skins, so sullen was his big face and so clumsy the finger that he thrust now and again into the little one's mouth to keep him quiet. And when he pulled the stopper out of the end of the bull's horn, he used a strength sufficient to tear an arrow out of the head of an elk. Nor had Tova or any of the others ever heard such lullabies, for their master sang the only songs he knew. They were gloomy war-songs which he had heard the vikings sing on calm nights as they sat at their oars and the lights of the coast of Frankland twinkled as distant and as tiny as the stars.

To such lays as these was Folke Ingevaldsson lulled into his first dreams as he sucked the rich yellow milk through the end of a bull's horn.

VIII

THE boy soon learned not to be afraid of his grandfather or his heavy-handed play, and an attachment grew up between them which was delightful to see.

Folke Filbyter always called him his son, as though Ingevald had never existed. He showed the women thralls that the boy had a little birth-mark in the shape of a star inside his left hand, and they thought this a good sign. When the sun shone, he tied him up in the skin bag and took him out into the fields; and they were never apart day or night. Where one was, the other was always to be found. If a child's cry was heard, one could be certain that it would be followed soon after by the deep man's voice which sounded like somebody talking in a barrel. The thralls called them "the pair of friends." With every rock that was rolled up the mount to the ring-work, with every arrow-head that was forged, they felt that now the new-comer was the most important person in the place and that everything was being done with his safety in view. They got into the habit of speaking of him as of a power that was present even in the remotest corners, and they thought a new era had begun with him. It was as though the little one hanging in his cradle from the sooty beam had already driven away some of the shame that lay upon savage Folketuna. Soon there was hardly one among them who would not have sacrificed his life for him with the incorruptible fidelity of a good thrall.

With Ingevald his father talked as little as before. Ingevald had no say in anything and no duties to perform. He no longer ventured into the woods without a body-guard of armed thralls, and in the presence of his child he felt strangely bashful and ill at ease. He always passed the cradle in silence, and often went a long way round to avoid it, and then he lay in the corner within the tent of skins with his face to the wall. As the thralls every evening, summer and winter, heaped the ashes over the embers on the hearth to keep the fire in, so he tried to save the last embers in his heart by hiding them every evening under his many bitter memories. But the flame would not be quenched; it shot up to the sky, and its glow grew deeper even than that of his love. Finally he lay all day long in a dull torpor. The thralls put their heads in and shook him, and they hung over him a sprig of mistletoe which they had found high up on an oak. "But you are past its help," they said. "It is as we guessed, you are smitten to death."

One bright sunny day the great plough was to be put into the ground. No one but the master might guide it, and for the first time he resolved to leave the boy for a while. He posted guards about the house and sent scouts up into the trees with strict orders to keep a sharp look-out.

He was still sitting with the child on his knee, unwilling to leave, but at last he rose on hearing a cry from his watchmen. And soon after there was a knocking on the door-post. It was old Jakob, and he hurried into the hall in his usual fashion, taking a long step across the threshold.

"A blessing on you all, dear friends," was his greeting. "I have often longed to meet you once more. But what has befallen my young brother, that he lies there so cast down? Even from here I see his weary face through the curtains. Now I perceive that I come at the right time, and I thank Thee, Lord, for guiding my footsteps."

"Your lord would do better to keep you at work instead of letting you roam idly about," replied Folke Filbyter, darkening.

It annoyed him to see that the boy stretched out his arms as though asking to be carried to the new-comer. He replaced the child in the hanging cradle and tied its thongs tightly.

"You say you have come at the right time," he growled as he did this. "That may be so, since they say you preachers have charms against sickness. So take your place beside Ingevald if you have any care for your life, and do what you can while I mind the plough. When I come back, if I find him cured and on his feet, you shall find mercy at my hands. If not, you must know that we have an old score to settle, you and I. You need not try to get away. I have watchmen out on every side, and I shall send out good bows to the men I have posted in the trees. You have no staff with you to-day, Jakob, and perhaps your back feels the safer for that. But your old staff is not far away. We found it in the shrine and it hangs over the stable-door."

"Follow your plough, Father, in this fine harvest weather," Jakob answered, as he went and sat by Ingevald. "And I shall tend the wounds of this sick heart."

Folke Filbyter then took the thralls out into the fields, and the little one fell sound asleep in the cradle, warmed by the sunshine from the hole in the roof.

"Jakob!" whispered Ingevald, sitting up. "Whence did you get the strength to forgive me when I struck you? I have pondered over it for many a night. In my dreams I have so often seen you come back that I only wondered that you did not come before. And when I dreamed of you, you were always in a hurry, walking fast and looking ahead. I was afraid you would have no time for me. I was afraid you would only press your lips to my forehead as before and go your way. What am I to you? A wicked man whom you have forgiven. Even the thralls have little respect for me, for I have been sick and weakly all my days. They have looked on me as lower than themselves, though I was the son of their master. I may well ask why I was ever born. Let me kiss you, humbly on the hands, for I am base-born and my father is more robber than franklin and my home is a shame to the country-side."

"Wild Folketuna is a new-sown field," answered Jakob, "and what may grow there at the last none can foretell."

Ingevald held his hands fast. With a burst of impetuosity he told of Soldis and her death, of his father's sworn brotherhood with Elk the Club King, and of all that had taken place at Folketuna.

"Ah, if you could make a new man of me," he wailed, "so that I might be like a leafy grove where song-birds may twitter but no hawk may enter in! Little do I know of what you teach, nor is it of that I ask; for the gods are many, but the power of your God is shown by your being noble and good. Much can you do, Jakob, but for my misfortune there is no help. I shudder less for myself than for all that through me will come into the world. No man can free himself from the heritage of his birth, and at Folketuna no noble fruit will grow. I was concealed among your hearers that night by the stones of judgment when you blessed all around you, but I felt it was not for me you spoke. Nor was it for the child who sleeps yonder in the sunbeam. How dark and how red that beam shall be before evening!"

"You speak as one who is sick and weary, Brother," said Jakob. "All the weary speak as you. And therefore I would fain answer you in quiet and childlike speech, as one talks to the sick and weary. But you do not know what your words mean to me. Of all the complaints I have heard on my wanderings, none has terrified me more than this, which has slowly bent you to the ground and which I have heard from so many. We are the fruit of corrupt trees, they said to me, and for us there is no hope. I could not answer that what they told me was untrue, but neither could I say that it was true. Brothers are not like brothers, nor sons like fathers, for even if they are alike in many things, they are seldom alike in all. The very difference may be so clear to see that the nearest kinsman may be the worst enemies. Much is inherited, but the half is acquired. The air and the people about us, the speech that daily buzzes in our ears, all enters into us and becomes part of us. Give me a young man and let me have charge of him, and I am well assured I shall make of him almost what I will. A young soul is an empty lamp. It may be of poor material or of the best, but the brightness of its flame depends most upon the oil that is poured in. Are we not all descended from thieves and murderers? But our will can be so forged that arrogance is beaten into strength, and weakness into loving-kindness. I myself was exposed as a child and found by a pious priest on a pile of faggots in the woods, and I know nothing of my parents. Perhaps I should be filled with shame and sorrow if I met them, sinful wretch as I hold myself to be. But there is one good thing about me, Ingevald. I know that with all my frailty I carry a spark of a holy will, and it bears me onward as upon wings. And in terror I have read in St. Augustine of original sin; but, instead of convincing me, he caused me to doubt, and I have often grieved the brethren at Skara with my heresy. For I am only a poor vessel of the Church and they are far more learned than I. I cannot argue with them, I can but see and believe. Nor am I a prophet, Ingevald, but yet I think it likely that your seed, like that of others, will consist of both good and bad men. And even if ten of your son's descendants be lost and only one rise like a star, you will not have been born or lived your life in vain."

"And can such a thing happen? Do you believe it?"

"Give me your child and we will try whether it be possible or impossible. When did you see that the fruit resembled the pale and ugly seed that vanished in the earth? I shall keep the boy hidden from all and be a tender and watchful father to him, so long as my good Master lets me."

"You know, Jakob, that whatever you ask of me I must give. But have you nothing for me?"

"Can you ask? As though I had not read plainly in your heart what you most earnestly desire! Have you not just told me your whole life? Why did you steal up to the judgment-circle when I was preaching, why did you hurl the stone god into the fosse? And what new light was it that fell upon you when the transports of love with their flames and their remorse had awakened you? Your thoughts cried out only for Soldis. But when she paled away and rode into the pyre, they still cried out, though louder than before, without your knowing that the name they cried had changed into another's. He, that other, has sent me. And now I will dress you in the white shirt which I carry in my scrip to-day. When I left Skara, a brother advised me to take it with me, and since then I have felt continually that somewhere a great joy awaited me. The way was long and my feet grew sore, but now I see that I have reached the place. My spirit was oppressed when I prime-signed the thralls at the judgment-circle; I knew they would soon forget me again and that it is the masters who here determine their faith. But now I see that it was for you I spoke, for none but you, though I did not know it at the time. Ingevald Folkesson, I here clothe you in the white vadum, the snowy garment of baptism, before you appear before Him for whom you have longed in secret."

"Take hold of me and help me to rise, so that I may kneel," Ingevald begged. "I believe in your God, the White Christ, since He is merciful."

Jakob took out a little bottle of oil and anointed him on the breast and between the shoulders and then clothed him in the white vadum. Then he bent his head over the pitcher that stood beside his bed and baptized him with prayers.

Ingevald shivered under the cold drops that ran down his neck, but was thrilled with the most unspeakable joy. He felt weak and deprived of will, but raised by loving hands into such a sea of light that at last he felt absorbed in it and sustained by the power of other beings. Voices spoke to him from far away in the wide unknown world. It seemed to him that some of the voices were those of powerful lords or bishops, but others were those of women or even children. They all told him that he was no longer alone, but that they loved him and rejoiced in him, though they had never seen him and would never even hear of him. They would live on as a united band among the rest of the people, even if he himself vanished in torment and death. They gave him a share of their strength, and to him this feeling of having at last found peace was altogether new, but to the wandering preacher it was a familiar daily companion.

Therefore, guessing his thoughts, he bent down to him and asked: "May I bring greeting to the brothers and sisters wherever I come?"

"You may," answered Ingevald.

The old man then prayed over him and gave him the brotherly kiss. Then he went to the slung cradle and baptized the child. Even in his prayers he spoke in his usual rapid voice, not from indifference or irreverence, but because the zeal of youth burned in his words as in his footsteps.

"King of men!" he cried. "Lord of the earth! Grant that the miracle happen! Show us, show all Thy people, that none need grieve any more as he grieves who now kneels before Thy throne. Even though his descendants may trample on Thy Cross a hundred times, show us that a pure and ardent will at last may spring even from the seed of evil and be turned to bright holiness!"

Ingevald was still on his knees and it was long before he raised his face. The smoke from the hearth enveloped the cradle in clouds, and through the open door he could see his father and the thralls at work in the fields.

"My pious benefactor," he whispered, "time is short; the others may come back at any moment. We must think of the child. Here he is in no danger, it is true, and everyone takes care of him—it is only I who feel a stranger to the boy. But in Folke Filbyter's house he will bring about his own undoing. Therefore you must keep your promise, Jakob, and take the child at once out of this robber's den."

"I have no greater wish, and I shall hide him so well that nobody shall find the place of his concealment. Now I will go to the stable to choose a strong horse."

"But you must not go across the yard, Jakob. Remember that my father holds nothing in life so dear as this child. Everything around us is an incomprehensible riddle, Jakob. Who would have dreamt that he could attach himself to any living creature? Slip along by the wall, so that no one sees you."

"Ah, you do not know how a deed of love brings confidence and success," answered Jakob. "It is not easy to fail in a deed of love, my happy brother."

The old man walked straight across the yard, and he met no one, nor did any of the workers turn round. Ingevald had never seen them dig and plough with their eyes so fixed on the ground. Even the scouts in the trees lay at full length on the branches with their eyes upon the dark furrows.

The stable-door creaked and Ingevald rose in fright. He staggered to the cradle, but Jakob was in the stable making his choice among the horses. He laid a cloth on the back of the biggest and buckled on a strong pack-saddle with a girth. As he could find no bridle, he left the halter on and led the horse into the open air. There he let him graze, and dropped the halter-strap so that it trailed in the grass.

Ingevald expected every moment that the horse would neigh. In his exhausted state, he began to tremble when Jakob came back to fetch the child.

"The boy is still so young that he sucks from a horn," he stammered, placing the bull's horn in the child's hands. "Its name is Månegarm and there are runes upon it, but in your hands, Jakob, they will have no evil power. If you shake the horn, you will feel that it is still full of milk. I have closed the lid tightly and fixed the wooden plug in the point. Do you know how to nurse a child, Jakob?"

"I know not what I am to say to that; but if Folke Filbyter could learn it without help, I may also try. Now I need no longer travel alone on the long roads."

He wrapped the boy in the bag of skins and unfastened it from the beam. Ingevald was continually pulling at his arm, and, summoning all his strength, he almost pushed him towards the door.

"At other times you are always in a hurry, Jakob. What does it matter if the bag is not so well tied? Do you not see that the horse has stopped grazing? He is raising his head and beginning to twitch his ears. Ride, ride away quickly for the sake of my child!"

"How can you think a little one like this would bear to ride quickly?" said the new foster-father. "No, slowly and at a walk we must make our careful way. To-day I must learn patience, and that may be good for me. But I shall not take the usual road, you may depend on that. I shall turn off into the heather, where no one will see our tracks if we are pursued. And certainly we shall be pursued. It cannot be long now before the master is back, and that will be a bitter hour for you, Ingevald. Hide yourself within the tent and close your eyes in prayer."

When he had climbed on the horse with his light burden, he fixed his eyes on the dark patch of cloud that hid the sun.

"Grant that the miracle happen!" he whispered with growing warmth. "It may reveal itself, when the time is come, as quietly as the opening of a rose. I am no prophet, yet I hear a Voice answering me. It shall happen, says the Voice, if one day there is born a descendant of this boy who shall love a drop of wax better than a pearl."

He was so absorbed in his prayer and his thoughts that he forgot to nod farewell to Ingevald. At a slow walking pace he rode through the gate and turned off under the oaks, guiding his horse all the time by the halter. The scout in the nearest tree had fallen asleep and the watchmen at the fringe of the wood were gathering berries. Not till after Jakob had disappeared did Folke Filbyter tie the reins to the plough-tail and turn his face towards home. All the time he was ploughing, a plover had been hopping in front of the horses, and he had had his eyes fixed on it, wondering at its boldness. Now it had flown away, and his first thought was to listen whether the child was crying for him. Though he soon convinced himself that all was still, a vague uneasiness crept over him and he hurried across the yard with short, resolute steps. Suddenly he remembered that Jakob was there and that he was to be punished if he had been powerless to cure Ingevald. With this in his mind, he called to the bailiff and the housecarls to go in with him.

The cradle was the first thing his eyes sought, long before he reached the doorway. But the light was bad indoors. Not till he had hold of the door-posts was he sure that his eyes had not deceived him, but that the two leather straps hanging loosely from the beam were all that was left of the boy's cot. Clad in his white baptismal shirt, Ingevald lay in his tent behind the skin curtains, looking more like a dead man than a living with his closed eyes and clasped hands. If anyone had come and told the master of Folketuna in so many words what had happened, he could not have understood it more clearly. During his forays in southern lands, he had seen many die in their white vadum and he knew what it meant. As though by the light of a sudden flash of fire, he saw before him old Jakob with his oil and his baptismal water, and then flying with the child in his arms to save it for the new faith. It did not occur to him to ask any questions or to give any hurried orders, but he let the ꞏnts pass in inactivity, not taking his eyes from the empty ꞏꞏs. Below them there was a hollow in the earthen floor, made by himself when he sat by the cradle. It made him think of a plundered nest, and he burst into wailing. It was not weeping and it had no words. It was a complaint like that the hunter sometimes hears at night from distant lairs in the forest. It rose and sank, and now and again it was stifled and still. He began to walk in a circle about the empty place, heavily swaying like a she-bear whose cubs have been stolen. The thralls threw down their picks and spades and joined him to share his grief. It had never entered their minds that Folke Filbyter had a heart. And now it burned before them with such a flame that their own shrivelled hearts were kindled by it. They felt they were his children, his only help; they clutched at his clothes and pressed food and water upon him, seeking to console him in their simple way. His bare warrior's arms hung listlessly, and his hands, warmed but lately with his work, grew cold and dry. Even when he heard them taking out the horses, he did not understand what it meant. He let them dress and arm him as they pleased, with the byrnie and the sax-sword and the huge kettle-hat.

When at last he sat in the saddle and the bailiff handed him the reins, he set off at once as fast as the shaggy little stallion could carry his heavy, jolting burden. The thralls followed him, some running on foot, others mounted, most of them unarmed. They had forgotten their enemies and the possibility of attack and thought only of tracking on every side like hunting-hounds. They forced their way into bushes and brakes, scattered along different paths, and went from one homestead to another. And they sent word to Elk the Club King and his men, whose horns were heard all day around the swamp. But all their trouble was in vain, and when Folke Filbyter rode past the shrine for the third time, he reined in his horse.

He ordered the thralls to break up the shrines, one by one. They tore down the bark roofs, overthrew the posts, and chopped the images in pieces, both those of the Æsir and that of the Mother of Jesus. The horses trampled the broken gods under their hoofs and he addressed the fragments in words of scorn. They came as slowly as when he had thought beforehand of what he had to say, but now they flowed straight from his soul, and in their solemn deliberation they sounded like a prayer. And even if the whole world had been listening, he would have spoken just as slowly and said exactly the same.

"If you have the power to bend one hair of my head, why do you lie still? Why do you not rise and take vengeance? In your name, men rob and kill without the courage to confess they do it for their own delight. I have appealed to air and mist every time I have sacrificed to you. In prosperity it was not from you I got my land and my good fortune, and in adversity you gave me no help. Naught do you fear so much as men's witness. My corn will grow as before and my thralls will work as before, for they are good thralls and are careful to do the will of their master. When at last they lay me in the mound, they will bear witness that I learned a lesson from life and that I asked you for nothing and gave you thanks for nothing."

So long as the thralls were busy breaking up the shrines, they obeyed him with revengeful glee, but when they heard his words, they were afraid and began to steal away. At last there was no one left with him but the bailiff. He also was on horseback, and once more they took the way through the woods.

There was now only one homestead where no one had asked for news, and that was Ulf Ulfsson's.

It lay down on the plain, and from the hill-path they could see the houses and the leafy guardian tree. Folke Filbyter turned his horse and made straight for the place.

"You have lost your wits, master," said the bailiff. "In your grief you know not what you are doing. If you will throw away your own life and that of your best thrall, you have only to ride on as you ride now."

Folke Filbyter rode on in silence, but the bailiff thought he would surely change his mind if he found himself alone. So he dismounted, but stayed watching at the edge of the wood, though he knew he would be of little help, being unarmed.

Folke Filbyter scarcely noticed that the thrall had stayed behind. When he came to the homestead, the gate was ajar and he was able to push it open with his foot. Difficult and uncomfortable as he found it, he was thus forced to dismount unaided, and he tied his horse to the fence. No one was to be seen about the place. He heard Ulf Ulfsson playing the harp in the hall, and he listened with his shoulder resting against the projecting door-post.

The sound of the harp was like the murmur of surf on the strand, and when he had stood awhile listening unconsciously, he recognized the melody. It was the same rowers' song with which he used to lull the child to sleep, only it sounded far sadder on the strings and seemed like an endless lament. He leaned his head against the wall and stood thus while the harping swelled into an ever fuller tone, without a thought of either making himself known or taking care for his safety. Nothing had ever grown in his heart but weeds and thistles, and now that the fire of misfortune had burnt and cleansed it, it had the untilled fertility of virgin soil. Strange little flowers opened their eyes within him and began to shoot up thicker and thicker, till his once barren heart was like one great flower-bed. It would have puzzled him sorely if he had tried to put a name to these unknown visitors; but he did not tell them over in any feeling of joy, if indeed he noticed their presence. He merely began to wonder that everyone called him wicked, for that moment, when his first grief had passed, he was conscious of no wicked will.

"It may be you have sometimes done evil in the sight of others, Folke Filbyter," he said. "Why were you not punished then? Why has the punishment waited till now, when you would not injure a creeping thing?"

When at last he looked up, the harp was silent and Ulf Ulfsson stood in the doorway, bare-headed and with a bow in his hand.

His cheeks were as white as his hair and he made a half-pace forward and bent down to look under the kettle hat. Was it actually his stubborn and wealthy enemy who stood there at his door so broken and dejected? What could have happened since their last meeting?

"You need not doubt it," said the byrnie-clad figure without taking his arm from the door-post. "I am your neighbour from Folketuna, your worst enemy. Long have I waited for you and your sons, Ulf Ulfsson. Little did I think that I should be the first to come. If you are impatient, lay an arrow to your bow and shoot."

Ulf Ulfsson laughed hoarsely and flung the bow to his eye and aimed, but let it sink again. Many times he did the same thing, and then his enemy said:

"If you would rather use the sword, come out into the meadow and fight. But first you must answer me one question. Have you seen the Christian beggar who rode off with your daughter's child?"

Ulf Ulfsson dropped his bow and came so near that the two men could have caught each other by the belt. His hair fell over his eyes and with a shaking hand he pointed to the seat of turf under the guardian tree without being able to utter a word.

"He sat there with your daughter's child?" asked Folke Filbyter.

"What are you saying?" said Ulf Ulfsson at last. "My daughter's child? I have had spies out. I know that my daughter is dead and that you yourself sat rocking the child. . . . Ah, now I see it, now I see it. Yes, here on this turf Jakob sat and rested. He was tired and hot, and I filled the horn myself with fresh milk for the little one. He said he

had been given it by a dying man who had taken baptism.
More he did not say. I felt no desire for longer talk with this
preacher, though out of pity for the unknown child I could not
deny him a moment's rest. Nor did I think to ask him whither
he was bound. It is long since he rode away—I did not even
see in which direction. Had I but guessed what I know now!
Was that child my daughter's? Perhaps he is taking it to
Skara; but there the king is master, and he is a Christian. And
there are high walls of wood which will give no answer if we
stand outside and shout. And he may know of even better
hiding-places."

"And in all this time have you done nothing to get your
daughter back, Ulf Ulfsson?"

"Not a day nor a night has passed but my first and last
thought has been of her. But I am not rich like you and have
not many men like you, and I knew the fight would be a hard
one. Far from here I have another house, and there I collected,
in secret, men and weapons and horses. We have scarce allowed ourselves food and clothing so as to be able little by little
to arm the force yonder. To enter a suit against you at the
Thing would have been trouble wasted, but I made a league
against you with my other neighbours. And just as the net was
ready to be drawn tight—aye, just then came the news that my
daughter was no more. The proud message with its double
meaning, which she sent by her sister, still rings in my ears."

"And all this you tell me openly and in so many words, Ulf
Ulfsson! Your daughter you can no longer win back, that is
true, but do you not think of revenge?"

"When we heard of her death, my sons went to their ships
and they are now harrying in the West. Revenge, neighbour,
is a thing we men need not trouble about. Retribution comes
as surely as snow in winter. It belongs to powers who are
wiser and stronger than we."

"Then we have not much more to say to each other, Ulf Ulfsson. Take up your bow, or, if you prefer the sword, go in and
fetch it. No one awaits me at home this evening and I have
good time."

Ulf Ulfsson did not move or accept his challenge. He recov-
ered a shadow of his old measured dignity.

"For a man who supports himself so unsteadily against the
door-post, it is not the right time for a challenge," he said.

When he came to a homestead, he never went into the dwelling-house but sat down under the guardian tree and bewailed his lot. He always called up the sons and the thralls and examined their hands carefully, and this was repeated so often that at last they came to him without being called. At first it was only the little children he wanted to see, but, as the years went by, it became the turn of the half-grown boys and finally the young men. But at the same time he began to fear that he had been too easily satisfied and that his inquiries had not been searching enough. His superstitious mind suggested an obscure suspicion that perhaps the lost child might in some mysterious way grow more quickly or more slowly than others, or might even be disguised in woman's clothes. So that at last there was neither young nor old, man nor woman, who did not have to stop and show their hands. People grew used to his visits, as though it were his destiny to travel the roads for ever. They were no more surprised at his continually returning as soon as the snow was gone than at the cries of the kites or the budding of the trees. He was known all round the country, and when the woman of the house saw him outside the gate, she would say: "There is the unhappy Master of Folketuna riding about to look for his child."

If he was not out on his quest he thought he was wasting time in idleness. In the course of his roamings he often came to very distant regions and the people of Folketuna did not hear the familiar slow tramp of his ever-weary horse until the darkness of Yule was drawing nigh. Several times he had reached as far as Skara, but the priestly edifice was surrounded by an insurmountable spiked palisade, which people called a wooden wall. It was true there was a grated opening in the gate, but he always turned his horse as soon as he came to it. The thrall guessed that his master feared above all things the loss of his last hope and for that reason he never seized the knocker. Nevertheless the thrall on one occasion hurried forward unexpectedly and knocked as loudly as he was able. Folke Filbyter dropped the reins and sat his horse like one turned to stone.

It was a warm day and he had hung his iron hat on the saddle. A strong smell of incense met him from the grating and a serving brother inquired the business of the strangers. Soon he saw the handsome face of an old man turned on him in sharp scrutiny. It was the chief of the Christian teachers and he was called a bishop, but it was long before he could understand the thrall's questions and he answered with a foreign accent.

"I remember being told that before I came here there was a brother named Jakob. They said that one day he came on horseback with a child that scarcely looked a year old. But when the inquisitive crowd and some of the teachers collected about him, he raised the child in his hands and preached such heresies against original sin that the brothers found themselves obliged that very day to thrust him out of their community. So I have been told. They afterwards wept greatly over him and prayed continually for his soul. Whither he may then have turned his steps I know not, but he was always wont to sleep in barns and woods. I have heard that in the course of years he has been here many times, but me he has never visited."

As he spoke, the bishop eyed the stranger's peculiar dress, splashed with mud. And it did not escape him that the ugly and otherwise repellent face showed a passing touch of gentle sorrow and almost of meekness.

"You are a wild man and a heathen," he said. "Was it your child? You are unhappy. It may be that I could help you better if you would be christened. Think of it when you are in solitude. Whence come you?"

This was too many questions all at once and Folke Filbyter only answered the last.

"I am from a distant region in the East, where Elk the Club King and Folke Filbyter make the roads unsafe, so that nobody dares to ride unarmed."

"Then depart to your home in peace," said the bishop; "for now a pious chieftain named Inge is set upon the throne of Upsala. He is an honest West Goth and he has sworn by his kingship to force order and good morals upon the East Goths. They worship Frey only for the sake of meal, believing Christ to be niggardly with the crops. But tell them that in a rich soil like theirs Christ too can return sevenfold. I have heard of Folke Filbyter that he is a man of ill fame. It seems he has more stolen goods than would endow my poor new-built church. He causes godly teachers to be flogged and has thrown down the image of Jesu Mother. This have I heard through travelling chapmen. Well, well, maybe at heart he is no worse a sinner than any man among us. One man gathers gold by raiding in foreign lands, another by merchandise, a third by highway robbery. But such things cannot long continue. A great light has been brought from the East and there are already so many hands to protect its flame that no wind can now put it out. Give the robber this message from me, that if he do not shortly make amends and send rich gifts of atonement, it will be necessary to part his head from his neck by so much space as will give room for a sharp sword between them."

"I shall remember your words," muttered Folke Filbyter menacingly. "But before the Master of Folketuna accepts Christian morals you will have to blunt much iron."

After this talk his mood became yet gloomier; the thrall, on the other hand, plucked up heart and said:

"We must cease asking for the child. You have heard how all those who may know something answer cunningly of other things. Now I shall no more speak of the child and only ask for tidings of Jakob. I shall pretend that you are an old friend who would gladly help him and take him home with you."

The thrall went into every house in the street of the friendly town and spoke with pity of the outcast preacher. The people were of cheerful disposition and ready to talk, and he took good time. But before he had reached the last house he came back and took his master's horse by the bridle and led him forward with determined steps.

"I was sure that to-day at least would not be without its reward," he said. "But now let me direct. Hitherto it has been my part to follow in silence."

He continued to lead the horse at a brisk pace, and as the sun was beginning to sink, the road turned off past a knoll. It was thickly overgrown below with thorny bushes, but on its top stood a group of aspen-trees with trembling leaves.

"Here under the aspens it must be," said the thrall. "By drawing out a word in one house and a word in another I got the good wives of Skara little by little to describe the place clearly. Each of them thinks she was very close and careful for they could not tell how much we meant with our friendship for the old hermit. Yes, hermit is what they say he is now and this must be where he dwells. All we have to do is to find a path through the thorn brake."

He led the horse on to the grass and when he came to the back of the knoll, away from the high road, a path appeared, with steps leading up to a wooden cross and a little cabin roofed with turf. In front of the entrance sat Jakob mending his shoes, and so busy was he with his work that he did not notice the strangers.

"Have you the boy with you?" asked Folke Filbyter.

Jakob started at the deep voice and looked anxiously over the bushes on the other side, thinking the cry came from the road. Only when he turned round was he aware that the Master of Folketuna had found him.

"Nay, by Christ, I am alone," he answered in anxious haste. "What makes you ride here in the Skara lands? Give up looking for the child, for you will never find him."

"It is for you we come now, Jakob," said the thrall. "Folke Filbyter has taken pity on you and will have you with him. Now I am coming up with a piece of rope to fetch you."

"If I am all you seek, my mind is calmer. It was Ingevald who gave me the child. He begged me to take him. I am no thief. But I know, Folke Filbyter, that you claim the rights of a master over every living thing in your house. If it will give you any consolation, avenge yourself freely on me."

He ceased his work, put on the half-mended shoes and came down. Folke Filbyter had him tied to his saddle and made him walk beside his horse the whole way home.

When at last they reached the bridle-path through the woods above Folketuna, they met Ulf Ulfsson. He was also on horseback and neither would make way for the other. The horses stopped facing each other with hostile snorts.

"Make way there for the chief man of the place," said Folke Filbyter, and the two enemies stared stiffly into each other's eyes.

"No, you shall make way for your elder," answered Ulf Ulfsson.

Then Jakob ran between them, as far as his rope would let him, and held the horses apart.

"Never did I admit more dangerous men than you, Ulf Ulfsson, and you, Jakob, through my gate," said Folke Fil-

byter. "Why did you seek me in my lair? I never bade you
come. You took from me the child and Ingevald and my peace
of mind and made me lonely and shunned. You robbed my
home of all and left me naked before my thralls, and let me
keep nothing but the red gold and the silver."

Then Ulf Ulfsson bent his head slightly and rode aside
among the trees.

"Our way grows ever narrower, neighbour," he said. "We
must make way for each other, but we should do it without
words."

They disappeared in opposite directions in the dusk of the
forest and the sound of the hoofs was scarcely heard in the
soft carpet of pine-needles.

When Folke Filbyter arrived at home he had Jakob chained
to the wall by a clamp which was bent into an iron collar
and riveted fast. His place was in the middle of the hall, and
on some days the master passed him the leavings when he had
finished his meal, on other days he let him starve. He moved
his seat near enough to the wall for Jakob to smell the food,
and for hours at a time he sat staring at his prisoner in un-
broken silence.

One evening, when the meal had been served and the fire
on the hearth lighted up the whole hall, he said to him at
last: "Jakob, now it is time to speak. Where is my son?"

"In my heart, master. In my heart and my thoughts always.
More will I never tell you. I was too fond of the boy for
that. You may lay on me all the tortures in your power,
but I shall keep silence."

"Thralls!" then said Folke Filbyter, "heat up an iron on
the hearth and put out the beggar's eyes. He is not worthy
to look again on the glorious sun."

The bailiff did as he was ordered and heated an iron in the
embers. When it was white-hot he went up to Jakob, held
up his eyelids and blinded both his eyes.

"The evening is fair and bright with stars," said Folke Filbyter, offering Jakob the dish, which he did not touch. "If
you are of my mind, we will chat awhile. Maybe your memory
will clear, now that you are no longer confused by outside
things. Tell me, Jakob, do you know anything of my son?"

"I have a good memory, and I know I wished him well."

Folke Filbyter leaned forward and bent over him,

"What most oppresses me is that I cannot guess how it is with him. Even if I am never to see him again, I should go more calmly into the mound did I but know this. Perhaps he crawls about the floor of some cabin and is given blows and cuts, while I sit by my treasure-chests for which I have no use. Perhaps he is in good case and plays among friendly people and will grow up into a hero before whom the sons of Ulf Ulfsson will bow low. Then he will never have a thought for me, never be humbled by a memory of the home where I am growing old in misery—I who yet would give all I own for two grateful words of remembrance."

His pain prevented Jakob from answering, but the thralls laid a cloth moistened with cold water over his eyes, and then he said:

"It was my desire to transform him, to make him so unlike you that you might meet him without a thought of kinship. If I had had my way, who knows how far I might have gone! But your son is only a beginning, Folke Filbyter. He may live as long as you and have sons and grandsons."

"Then you believe he is still alive. With your half-told tale you would have me imagine I am punishing you unjustly."

"There was a time when I cursed the world's injustice, but I do so no longer. Nay, beat our bodies with the hard blows of thy wings, thou Unjust One, and wake us, wake us! I was strengthened even by the first blows I received at Folketuna, but never have I felt so strong as now. And what would have become of Ingevald if injustice had not pressed a thorn into his foot? Injustice is the harsh and prickly wood that must be piled up where the fire is to burn."

"If you confess what you know of my son, you shall receive a handsome reward instead of punishment and injustice. And you shall have the thanks of a broken man."

"It is only evil that is rewarded, master. Learn to live so that you can never receive full justice.—Gregory the Great of Rome writes: No pope has done more for the Church than I, and therefore I must fall.—That was rightly written, Gregory. He whose acts are good shall be called evil, and the best shall be called the worst. They shall be called the worst even by those who know well in their hearts that it is a lie which cries to heaven. How would life look here on earth if the good lost their belief in punishment and began to count on profit even as the wicked do? Then good would be a greater evil than evil itself. Rewards are the work of men, and with them they seek to their own perdition to shake the foundations of injustice. See how everything great shrinks in size when it is rewarded after its deserts, but that which perishes in injustice continues to cry, eternally young, from its grave. Injustice is the profoundest and holiest element that was instilled into creation in order that strong beings might arise."

"Yet Ulf Ulfsson seems to think I suffer justly," said Folke Filbyter, thrusting aside his untouched meal.

"I think so too. Ulf Ulfsson had no evil intention when he first entered your house, and yet he was afflicted like you. No one has striven for your son's welfare as I did, and now I sit here blinded and in pain. It seems to me that we all three suffer justly, but perhaps there lies on the surface of our cup a drop of injustice. And it is that drop which keeps us alive."

"You are a more dangerous man even than Ulf Ulfsson. It is a danger to my house to have you chained to the wall. I have burnt away your sight so that your eyes are dried up and shrivelled. Will you force me to take away your tongue too? Fetch the wool scissors, bailiff, and cut off his tongue!"

Jakob sat on the floor with his neck against the wall without moving.

"You will free me from a grievous temptation. To know that you are so sorely afflicted and to hear your questions without making answer is the greatest temptation that God has yet put upon me. I am bound by an oath. Poor master, I may not help you."

"Bailiff, let the scissors alone," said Folke Filbyter, and the thralls began as usual their well-meaning efforts to console him with food and drink.

"Where are his sons?" they whispered one to another. "What will happen now, what will become of Folketuna?"

No more was said that evening, and whole weeks might go by without a single word being addressed to Jakob. Now and then Folke Filbyter threw him a bone or reached him the dish, and then his chain rattled as he moved on the floor with his elbows.

Folke Filbyter left off counting days and years. There was no measurer of time about the place except the cock, who crowed on his beam at midnight and sunrise, but took no account of the changes of the moon or of the seasons. Nor was there any rune-staff on which to cut marks, for runes had always been feared there as magic signs and sorcery. All they knew was that summer was coming on when the fields grew green, and the winter was at hand when the snow fell. Therefore no one could say with certainty how many years had gone by since the misfortune had fallen upon them. Some guessed twelve years, others twenty. The older thralls began to die off. The younger told tales of Jorgrimme's daughter and of the horn Månegarm, without believing in them. If the master himself spoke of old days, it sounded like a distant voice from the wilds, where the wanderer takes clouds for mountains and meadows for lakes. His riches increased continually and filled more and more chests, which were nailed down when full and never again opened. During the long winter evenings he sat among the cinders with empty hands, saying nothing, and grew old but could not die.

X

EVENSONG was just concluded in the Varangians' church of King Olaf the Saint at Micklegarth, and their captain, who sparkled with jewels from his shoulders to his belt, was forming them into the different guards for the night.[12] One party was in full dress like himself and marched up to the palace to stand on guard outside the Emperor's door.

"Remember!" he said. "Helmet on even when asleep, shield over your breast, sword under your head and hand on the hilt!"

The rest he dismissed to the Varangians' quarters and they were free until the midnight bell. Gaily they threw their arms about one another's necks and began to sing the tune of a Northern dance, but were often obliged to break the chain, for the church was only half built and the scaffolding was in their way. The moonlight came in among the unplaned, whitewashed beams, but it was not like the moonlight at home, which clutched at the heart and pressed it till it could scarcely beat. It was not dull and dead like the night of the last day, but it bathed the city and the men's faces in a light which forbade all dreams but of women.

And it was of women they sang, as they rejoined their long lines and brought their feet down with a mighty stamp on the flat stones. Beside the great square lay a tavern whose open roof was reached by a flight of steps overgrown with roses and myrtles, and a lofty cypress threw its slender shadow across the road. Here they had to break the chain again, as the steps were narrow. They put down their sharp battle-axes and wiped the dust from their feet. Lamps were hanging on the roof and a row of Greek girls leaned over the railing and greeted them with laughter. In the middle of the space, which was walled only on three sides, sat the owner of the tavern with a few other men, warming their feet at a

---

[12] Micklegarth was Constantinople, and the Varangians were the famous body-guard, composed of Scandinavians of good birth, who attended the Eastern emperor.

brazier. Their talk was very animated, for like all Byzantines they were engaged in a theological argument.

"I tell you," the host insisted, interrupting sharply, "that whatever your faith you will always be an infidel to some other man. When I was a prisoner of Alp Arslan I was called an infidel because I did not believe in the seven heavens and the Prophet of Mecca. But what could I say on my side of Alp Arslan or of the Jew who shared my prison and woke me every morning by calmly denying the Holy Virgin in a loud voice? And these Varangians, who have been my good customers and brothers from of old, they tell me that in their country a man is called infidel if he does not slaughter a boar every Christmas. No, my friends! My belief is this, that my tavern will always be the heaven where all disputes are drowned in a cup of well-spiced wine."

He sprang up as actively as he was able and his ample cloak dragged about him on the carpet. Thrusting his hand into his pocket, he brought out a pair of dice which he threw down on the table. Then he took the girls by the waist and threw them one after the other into the arms of the approaching Varangians. White as marble in the moonlight they gave the bearded warriors smacking kisses on lips and cheeks and drew them to the sofa. Their black hair was loose and their arms and shoulders, which were rubbed every morning with a paste of wheaten bread and asses' milk, were as soft to the touch as rose-leaves. On their foreheads they wore a gold fillet with a green stone. But there were many of them, and those who were left over set about the food. They boiled raisins, plums and cherries with honey and cedar-water and sprinkled little tarts with oil of aniseed. As the dishes were ready they set them out on a three-cornered cloth which the host spread on the floor, as he bustled about, continually catching his feet in his cloak.

Meanwhile two Varangians had seated themselves at the table with some gold coins before them and were throwing dice. No sooner did one win than at the next throw his winnings returned to the other. They eyed each other with black looks and for a while the dice lay untouched.

"What is the use of this everlasting game?" the younger at last exclaimed, thrusting aside the dice. "It never leads to anything, and after all we are sons of the same father."

Instantly all the Varangians rushed forward, freeing themselves from the arms of their temptresses as nimbly as a vinedresser bends aside the clinging tendrils. They bent over the boot, examining it and feeling it cautiously, as though reverence forbade them to touch it, and at last they even kissed the gold eagle.

"God have mercy on this sinful city!" they muttered. "It is the Emperor's!"

"Yes, it is the Emperor's," answered the messenger, still panting. "You know the sign? You remember what it means when his purple boot is thrown to the Varangians?"

"The Emperor is dead!"

"You all know that he has long been ailing. The priests forbade him to drink wine and the physicians to drink water. Therefore this evening he ordered sherbet to be brought. What was at the bottom of the cup perhaps his inconsolable consort could tell us, or maybe the holy Patriarch, but we Varangians know nothing. And we wish to know nothing."

"No, we will know nothing. We only know that when the Emperor's purple boot is thrown to us Varangians it means we have a right to the Polota Svarv."[13]

"It means that now we shall be rich," said the messenger, but they all descended the stairs in solemn silence, for the Emperor had shown them favour and they were devoted to him.

Each man sought out his weapon from among the axes standing against the wall, and it was easy to recognize the marks in the moonlight. It almost seemed as though they were ashamed to hurry, so slowly did they cross the square; and many times they stopped and spoke to one another in hushed voices. Ingemund and Hallsten were whispering that the same ship which had brought them still lay in the harbour, though with patched sail. Now and then a stifled lament came from the tavern above their shining silver helmets, otherwise there was no sound but of hurrying footsteps. They met a stream of courtiers who disappeared into the cathedral, where the lamps were lighted around the marble columns from Ephesus.

"Varangians! Varangians!" they cried at last, as they

[13] *Polota-svarv* means literally "palace-scouring." This right of the Varangians is referred to in Harald Hárdráde's Saga.

thundered with their axes upon the iron gate of the palace, which instantly opened as though of itself.

The outer court was full of guards. A black slave-boy stood by the fountain holding a torch above his woolly head and weeping. Farther on, the Varangians saw that the gate of the inner court was ajar and that torches and lanterns were moving in all directions. Then all at once they increased their pace and ended in a run.

"Varangians! Varangians!" they howled, cutting blindly about them with their axes, so that some of them stuck fast in the stems of the cypresses. They burst into the inner court like a lot of starving lions and bears let loose in the circus. All those they met gave way, hiding behind curtains and statues. Still shouting their "Varangians! Varangians!" they hurried through the colonnades into the narrow treasury, where their chief stood waiting for them.

"Every man has the right to take as much as he can carry away in his hands," he said. "Only what lies within this iron cage no one may touch, for there are the sacred lily diadem and the rose diadem, and they are imperial heirlooms. Remember now! Nothing on your backs, nothing under your cloaks! All you take must be carried in front of you."

"You need not tell us, we have been here before!" cried some of the oldest, pushing him aside. They stood upon tables and benches to reach the higher coffers and the richly ornamented saddles and horse-cloths. Some took clothes, armour and costly weapons, but the majority plunged their hands into the chests of loose pearls and stones of every kind. The treasury officials stood as though nailed to the walls and had voluntarily left the keys in all the locks.

"You are late, Varangians," said their captain, who had already helped himself to a heavy staff of gold. "We must make haste. It is the turn of the courtiers next."

They loaded their hands with as much as they could hold and then marched out with the gleaming booty held before them. The Folkesons were the last to leave. Ingemund had chosen rings and coins and such things as were of pure gold, but Hallsten could not make up his mind and had only collected a few pearls.

"I am looking for something more valuable than gold and

them wanted to be left behind, but each wanted the other to stay. The end of it was that the sail flew up the mast again.

When they anchored by Niörva Sound they heard that the Norsemen had long since returned to the North. So they set out on the great salt sea and steered for the winter nights.

It was a hard voyage, for three men had always to sit at the steering-oar and the others were fully occupied in bailing. Only when off the English coast did they sight a fleet of about forty vessels. One ship was larger than the rest and bore gilt ornaments; the gaping dragon's head and tail were both covered with gleaming scales. On the poop stood a broad-shouldered man with the ensign of a chief. It was fastened to a pole like other chiefs' ensigns, but it was neither of gold nor silver nor wood nor cloth; it was of wrought iron and represented a coiled snake raising its head towards a star. The Varangians took it for a symbol of wisdom and thought it might well suit Blot Sven.

To make themselves known they began a song in the Goths' tongue. They were answered at once in the speech of Swedes and Norwegians and then they lowered their sail and rowed in among the ships. They were well received and were given bread baked with blood and many other Northern dainties for which they had longed for years. Then they joined Sven and won renown and riches, and Ingemund and Hallsten were soon reckoned among the chief of his men.

Finally it came about that the fleet lay for a whole week waiting for calm weather in order to hold a Thing in open sea. During the whole voyage the crews of the different ships could only communicate with each other now and then by shouts or by swinging a torch. But a red cloak hoisted in the leading ship told them that a Thing was to be held and that they were not to lose sight of each other unnecessarily. They were hungry for news and overjoyed when at last a dawn brought calm. Ships' tents and sails were taken down and all the forty vessels rowed up to their leader and lay in rings, one outside another, the biggest and most splendid ships inside and the smaller outside. Gangways were made fast between the gunwales so that men could pass to and fro as on bridges in a floating town. As soon as all was in order they washed their faces and arms and put on full armour as though for battle. Those who had not yet polished their helmets and byrnies made haste to rub and scour them. There was great talking and jesting, and the boundless ocean lay bright as a mirror with no sign of land.

Sven, who was an old and sombre chief, had already mounted the poop. It was his way to stand there watching the constantly changing shapes of the clouds. His grizzled beard was made up of an immense number of little round close curls, and his hair was the same. As he stood bare-headed it was like an ice-grey cap of skin fitting closely to his crown. His bulging forehead stood out above his little deep-set eyes, but the lower part of his face receded and his nose was small and straight. A more melancholy pair of dreamy eyes had never gazed over the sunny sea; their colour shifted like that of iron, between grey and black and blue. So it was also with the faded cloak which he wore over his shirt of mail; some called it grey and others black. But his face and his slender weatherbeaten arms were of a deep ruddy hue, the result of many years' exposure to sea salt.

The clouds drifted across the sky like little lambs and piled up their masses into high mountains or images of gods or floating worlds with trees and towns. When Sven had watched their movement for a while, he closed his eyelids tightly and compressed his lips.

"Why does not Hallsten Folkeson come?" he asked Ingemund, who stood by him.

"Truly, chief, I might ask that question myself," he answered sharply, and his moustache bristled haughtily. "But if you will answer me another question, tell me what wonders you are looking for in the clouds."

"I am waiting," said Sven. "I am waiting for my fate, and our fates are like the fickle shapes of the clouds. It is chance that determines our meetings, our love and friendship, our misfortunes and enmity. Even the gods must bow before the Fates. Much have I learnt, and I am assured of the mutability of all things. I have ceased to prophesy and hope. I wait."

"Then why do you ask after my brother?"

"Because the men are ready to open the Thing."

"As I have told you already, chief, Hallsten asked for the loan of our ship for two days, but I could not get him to give any reason. I came aboard your ship and saw that he steered towards the Orkneys. He knew well enough that we were only waiting for better weather to hold the Thing, and with his fifteen pairs of oars he ought to be able to keep his word in spite of the calm. I am sorry I agreed to his request, for he is so thoughtless that he needs a cool head to advise him. But there is no help for it now, and we must hold the Thing without him."

"Without him! Nay, Ingemund. He is one of our best men, though he has let himself be christened like you and many more. For besides wild men from Halogaland I have with me Christians from the Trondelag and Danes and Goths." With a friendly but bitter smile he clapped Ingemund on the shoulder and added: "Those who seek power and honour know what they have to do in an age when every king accepts baptism."

"There is a thing called faith, chief."

"Not for young men whose hearts beat so impatiently as yours. To you two brothers the world will remain yet awhile the unplundered treasury of the King of Greece. You are wild and full of your own affairs and have skulls harder than a buck's. What does it trouble you to-day whether at the last the god of death be the one-eyed Father of the Æsir or another? What is it to you whether it is the long-legged Hönir with his storks who runs round and leaves the babies in people's houses or whether it is Saint Nicholas with his staff and his pail of water? Do you always remember, when you make your deepest reverence, whether it is the sign of Thor or of Christ that you draw over your heart? The gods are for us old men, and I rejoice in your young strength. In the memory of man no viking fleet so great as mine has been under sail, and I feel that it will be the last. It was a lucky chance for you to join it. You have luck, you sons of Folke, and you will go far—if you do not kill each other."

"You mean something by your last words."

"Else I should hardly have spoken them."

"You mean more than you say."

"Maybe. I am on the track of a secret."

He sat down on the bench, but his men were impatient and turbulent.

"The wind may freshen again at any moment," they grumbled. "It is not fitting to wait for so young a man. Besides, we know that newsmen have arrived and we want to hear what messages they have brought."

"Why does Hallsten delay?" asked Sven, turning again to Ingemund.

"Ah, answer that who can."

"And what if I can answer better than you, Ingemund?"

"Still I shall doubt to the last."

"Yet you know that Hallsten used to sit with me in the ship's tent in the evenings. It passed the time to listen to him and I am so used to his company that I miss him now."

"And what secrets had he to disclose?"

"Little enough, you may think, and yet much for an old man who only has his sword for a bedfellow."

A gleam of uneasiness troubled Ingemund's eyes.

"Has he spoken about our home?"

"Of your father he has not said much."

Ingemund grew calmer.

"Our father is a rich udalman of the old sort—a good heathen."

"I'm glad, I'm glad. Hallsten has always been shy to speak of him, but I have coaxed out of him a word or two about your games and pastimes when you were young. Is it not true that unknown to your father you used to steal away to the woods and play with a little golden-haired maid from the neighbouring manor?"

"Ah, there I hear Hallsten speaking. He is one of those who would do well to eat a wolf's heart now and then."

"Did she promise to wait for you?"

"We were children and only spoke in play."

"And afterwards you both held fast to the memory of her. She must be a fair grown-up woman now, Ingemund."

"Indeed, she can scarcely be called young any more."

"A ripe woman is held in great esteem at home. I have heard of women being carried off when their hair was already grey. But how can you be sure she is still waiting for you?"

"Of that indeed we know nothing, but suitors are rare in our part. And if she is a wise woman she will understand that an alliance with her nearest neighbours will suit her best."

"Maybe you are right there, and the women at home are a patient race."

Ingemund drew back with a smile.

"I came to hold Thing with you, chief, and little thought

that at your years you could be so curious about our love fancies."

"True; but then you would have news of Hallsten's doings."

"I cannot see the meaning of all this."

"But to me it seems clearer and clearer. What was it she was called, your neighbour's daughter?"

"Holmdis was her name."

"Aye, Holmdis was her name. It had slipped from my memory, but that is the name I heard. And is it not true that you often speak of her and that neither of you will give way?"

"Once more, chief—I came to your ship on other business. If you wish to know it, what you say is true. But is it to make a fool of me that you talk so loudly of all this?"

"Listen now, shipmen, it was true! I have taken a liking to the two sons of Folke and am minded to brush aside the shadow which in your eyes has lain upon them, since you found they were charged with a common secret. Now the veil is torn aside. The two brothers are suitors to the same woman. Is that a thing to hide or to blush for?"

Ingemund flared up.

"As good brothers we have promised each other to hold together in friendship and on our return to contend for her in free rivalry with our gifts. Ulf Ulfsson, her father, is of old lineage and will make a hard bargain over his daughter's bridal."

Sven continued his questions.

"What gifts does Hallsten bring?"

"None as yet, so far as I know. The proud fellow has thrown away everything, thinks nothing good enough. Even in the treasury of the Greek King, where he would keep nothing but a few jewels for his shoes and clothes. But what right have you to examine me thus closely in the hearing of all your men?"

"You shall soon learn my reason, Ingemund. And yourself, what gifts do you bring?"

"I have kept to pure gold," replied Ingemund with growing resentment, resolved to answer no more questions. "If you wish to see, I have melted it down into two thick rings, so soft that a strong woman can bend them and so heavy that they outweigh my sword. Here they are, hanging in my belt."

Sven felt the rings and the sword.

"A light sword and heavy gold rings to weigh against each other," said he. "But how is it with your sword, Ingemund? It is indeed far lighter than the gold, nay, almost as light as the skirt of your cloak."

Ingemund said nothing, but in his anger he suddenly plucked the sword from its sheath and held it before Sven's eyes.

"It is wood!" he said. "Are you satisfied? By God, I had rather let a few enemies escape with their lives than cut down my own brother in a heated moment."

"Such envy and such friendship between these two brothers! Now you have all heard it. That was the secret. But can I believe my eyes?—there is a sail!"

"It is hard to sail in calm water," said Ingemund mockingly, but on turning his head he saw there was indeed a ship approaching. She was sailing far off in a fresh breeze, which swiftly rippled the surface of the sea, and he recognized Hallsten's sail by its yellow stripes.

As soon as the vessel had come alongside the outermost ring of ships, Hallsten hastily jumped on board the next vessel and ran towards the chief's ship across the swaying gangways. He was easily known by his silver helmet with its crest of a golden fish and by his flowing hair. The nearer he came, the more brilliantly sparkled his Varangian dress with the jewels which he thought too easily come by to be saved, but yet too tempting not to be worn. He hurried towards Sven, and now it could be seen that Hallsten's costly dress was in tatters. One of his knees was bare and bleeding, the skin was torn from his elbows, and two rusty iron rings hung at his belt.

"I am late, I know, but I did it!" he said gaily, showing his bandaged hands.

"Is it these iron rings that you think of offering to Ulf Ulfsson and his daughter?" asked the chief.

As Hallsten looked about him in surprise and hesitation, he added:

"I scarcely thought it was anything so mean you went to seek. But now tell me and my men your adventures. You need hide nothing, for I have told them all; and though at first you may think I have done ill, you will soon be of another mind. They know that you brothers are courting the same woman with your gifts and that her name is Holmdis."

Hallsten looked doubtfully at his brother.

"You have had so little care of our secret that there is not much left to hide," said Ingemund, still red in the face with anger.

"Shipmen!" cried Hallsten, light-heartedly suppressing his embarrassment; "you know the story of Olaf Tryggvason. He was the greatest of athletes and did not shrink from climbing the dizziest crags to hang his shield on them. One night our chief told me he had himself seen the rusty remains of an iron chain which this daring climber had once made fast high up on a cliff in the Orkneys. Since then I knew no rest, for I saw that this was the treasure I so long had sought, the treasure that was worth more than gold. Therefore, without confiding in any man, I steered for the cliff. It was a marvel that I found any hold for feet and hands on the sheer wall of rock, and when I had got the iron rings on my wrist I lost my grip and fell. If the sea had not been deep and free of rocks I should not be standing here with my prize."

Sven's stern weatherbeaten face brightened for a moment and he looked kindly at Hallsten.

"Would all my men were as you! But what do you want with these common iron rings?"

"Now I can go home with an easy mind, chief. If Ulf Ulfsson's daughter sets more price by the gold, then I know that in any case I would not have her, even if she gave herself for nothing."

Ingemund's fingers were playing with the hilt of his wooden sword. In his anger he forgot his usual taciturnity and exclaimed aloud with scorn:

"To speak the truth, brother, for us sons of Folke a marriage with any of the Ulfungs' honoured race would be good enough, were it won with gold or iron."

"You look upon this woman with different eyes," said Sven, interrupting, and he ordered the trumpets to call the men to his standard. "Therefore your grief will be different when one of you loses her.—The Thing is opened. Let the newsmen who sailed hither from Svithiod stand forth and speak."

There was a movement in the ship that had lately arrived and lay next to the chief's. It could be seen that most of those on board were peaceful envoys and only a few were armed like vikings. Two of them wore chain-mail even over their faces, leaving only their eyes uncovered, and they went aboard the chief's ship.

"We are the sons of Ulf Ulfsson," said he who stood on the right. "We have already made this known to you, chief, and now we thank you for what you have let us hear and see to-day. Know, you children of shameless Folketuna, that for your sake we are come hither. Off Lindesness we met the envoys' ship and heard that you were here, and then we came with them to challenge you to single combat and to be revenged on your race. But you seem to be better men than your kinsfolk, and we would challenge no guiltless men. We too practise Christian customs."

"What has happened, then?" asked Hallsten, moving towards them; but they checked him by laying their hands on their swords.

"We are not such good friends that we have any desire to talk with you. You will come home soon enough, and till then you may thank God for every hour you pass in ignorance."

Sven stood biting his lips and blinking.

"We have more important business," he said. "Return to your ship, Ulfungs. Your swords are still thirsty and rattle in their scabbards; if you stay too long you will not be able to keep them quiet. It is time for the envoys from my brother-in-law, King Inge, to appear, and I see them throwing off their warm furs. But it wants a strong and practised voice to make oneself heard at sea, so I shall speak in their stead. Perhaps I ought to be glad to sit next the King's seat at the Yule feast as his brother-in-law, but rather would I sit in it myself. Then we should once more make solemn vows over the festal cup. We Norsemen have taken towns and castles on every coast, but instead of setting up our own gods there, we have brought home those of the vanquished. You will find it hard to believe the news I shall now give you. The mighty Emperor of Saxland has crossed the mountains, an outlaw, barefoot in the snow, and gone to Canossa to beg pardon of the Pope.[16] To this it has come with the lords of the earth.

---

[16] Saxland was at this time the Scandinavian name for the whole of Germany. Any country south or south-west of Germany was called indiscriminately Valland, or "foreign parts."

Inge sends word that men shall go no more a-viking in summer, but instead shall pay him tribute and give tithes to the Pope. He orders you to return and says that if you come at once he will accept the best of you in his body-guard. If there is any man among you whose spirit is still defiant and who will stay at sea with me, let him raise his sword!"

Not a man drew his sword and a deep silence reigned. Sven pressed his curly beard against his chest and closed his eyes, as though to listen the better to the sting in his own voice.

"A vikings' Thing seldom passes off as quietly as this. My luck is out and distrust surrounds me. When as a boy I went to play and asked who would come with me, there was the same silence. Now my men are tired and begin to take thought for their old age. There is nothing to do but draw in the gangways and row the ships apart and set a course for the home skerries. I am a deposed chief, for being faithful to the old gods."

He opened his eyes on hearing the sudden noise of the men hurrying back to the outer ships. As the oars were put out he gazed at the clouds, whose light and fugitive forms were mirrored in the sea.

XI

I T was pitch-dark and a line of torches moved through the forest, one after another; there seemed no end to the procession of wandering flames. They burned still and clear, for the weather was calm. Now and then they were screened by a hand, as a gust came in the tree-tops, and then their light shone upon stern and serious faces. It was Inge's bodyguard and his chaplains who were carrying Ulf Ulfsson with them into the woods, his hands bound with a rope. Beside him walked Inge's Earl, a young cleric whose place was by the King's prayer-stool rather than in his armoury, and who had the look of a monk in his simple black frock. His hair had a gleam of red in it and a shrewd, dry uprightness showed in his lean and harsh features.

They went deeper and deeper into the forest until they had left all human habitations far behind. Then at last all the lights gathered about the dead trunk of an oak, and to it Ulf Ulfsson was bound fast.

The Earl stood before him and looked him in the face.

"I know they call me an oppressor of the people," he said, "because I turn Inge's circuit of the realm into a triumphal progress of the new faith. I know too that you are the most respected franklin in the district. I would rather spare you, but someone must be made answerable and we are too few to overcome the wild robbers who have entrenched themselves on a knoll not far from here. You have said that your gods dwell by the springs and among the trees of the forest, and now I commit you to them to perish of hunger and cold."

Ulf Ulfsson stood calm and motionless by the tree-trunk, through shrivelled by age and bent by troubles. He met the eyes of the Earl with such firmness that the King's powerful minister was forced to look aside, and then he said:

"When Loki reckons his cunning plans on his fingers he does it so eagerly that his fingers change their skin according to his thoughts. Now they are sheathed with the smooth scales splendid Varangian dress. As soon as the ship touched land they had jumped ashore and set out on their journey. Their object was to overtake Inge on his royal progress and be admitted to his famed body-guard before the rest of the crews had had time to draw up their ships and rest themselves at Lödöse. They walked in silence side by side, busy with their thoughts and hopes.

Suddenly the sound of hoofs was heard upon the rocks far off. At first it was like a stray horse recklessly tearing over stocks and stones. Gradually the tramp came nearer and nearer through the forest, evidently following the straight and open path. The jingling of little bells such as were worn on bridles suggested that there was a hand which held the reins. The two men therefore drew their swords, and Hallsten, who never refused danger, placed himself astride the path.

Ingemund pushed him aside.

"You have the tinder," he said. "I will see to the rest."

Hallsten had barely time to take out the tinder, which he carried in a walnut stuck together with wax. It had become damp from the warmth of his body and he had to strike the flint seven or eight times before he got fire. By that time the horse was upon them and reared on seeing them in the dark. For a second, Ingemund had a glimpse of the black snorting head against the stars and was able to catch the bridle.

"What do you want with me?" cried a ringing woman's voice. "Are you some more of Inge's men?"

"Inge's men? Is he so near?" asked Ingemund. "No, we are not yet his men, but if God will, we soon shall be. Why such haste, Valkyrie?"

"I am not bound to give you a reason."

"Men who walk the lonely woods would fain know what goes on in the world. Whence come you?"

Hallsten had now got the waxed wick alight and in its gleam the brothers distinguished two heavy plaits of hair and a blue kirtle rucked at the knee, for the woman rode astride. But of her face they could not see much, as she at once began to cut at Ingemund's arm with a little ax, and each stroke threw her head into shadow. The ax could not bite on the shirt of mail, but the pain of the blows angered him and he raised his sword in defence. At the next cut it flew in pieces and only a jagged stump of wood was left in the hilt. Greatly surprised, she ceased her strokes; at the same moment the taper burned out and Hallsten had not another with him.

"They were right at home," she exclaimed, "when they teased me for knowing so little of the ways of strangers. Now I have learnt that mail-clad warriors can stoop to attack a woman, but that they fight with wooden swords I should never have guessed."

"And I hope I shall not need so brittle and harmless a weapon much longer," Ingemund answered, as he threw away the empty hilt. "Is it far to Ulf Ulfsson's house?"

"Ulf Ulfsson's house! I come from there, but I scarcely know whether it is his any more, so crowded is it to-night with guards and men-at-arms."

"Did you fly because they were so many?"

"No, not that, but because King Inge is there."

"Where the King is, there should be safety."

"Why, do you not know that Inge is the most dangerous woman-hunter in the whole country?"

"You are afraid he will carry you off."

"No, Inge does not carry off women. King Inge has no need for that. He captures them with his eyes and his fair words."

"And he tempted you?"

"No, no, not that either, but he let the Earl take my father away, I know not whither. The Earl, who is a hard and cruel man, would force baptism upon him, and when he refused he was led away. Inge sat in the high seat, blushing and saying nothing—and for that I will no longer show him the courtesies of hospitality."

"You might have stayed and turned your back on him."

"You may say that, who have never met him. No one turns his back on Inge. It is no easy thing to show him an unfriendly face, and therefore I took horse and fled. He is as brave and gay and radiant in the high seat as Thor himself, and the clasp of his hand is as hearty. There are many sayings about him, but the commonest is this: When Inge laughs the whole world smiles!"

Hallsten then came forward to her horse.

"Your father—is he Ulf Ulfsson?" he asked; but his voice

XII

INGE sat in Ulf Ulfsson's high seat, youthful, beardless, radiant with goodwill and regal pomp. His coat of mail was all of silver and his light-blue tunic was embroidered with silver falcons with outstretched wings. He was holding a carouse with men and women, and now and again he leaned forward like a young lion ready to make a spring.

He took with him on his royal progress a cock in a gilded cage and two women, whose names were Julia and Julitta. The cage was hung before his closed bed, so that the cock might wake him by his crowing at midnight and at dawn for the appointed prayers; for Inge was a great hunter and came home tired at evening, but was none the less eager in his devotions. Julia was his mistress and Julitta her sister. Julitta was poor in outward seeming, being small and thin, but she accompanied her elder sister from devotion and admiration, and served her as a voluntary thrall. She was lively and quick of speech and entertained the King and all his court with her wit. She now stood at the end of the table telling stories, with her elbows in to her sides and her hands spread out. Julia sat smothered in jewels with the King's arm round her shoulders, playing with his fingers or drinking lip to lip with him from the horn. It was a curious horn, a present to Inge from his Earl. It stood upon wolf's feet made of iron and many runes were carved on it; it was said to have belonged to the dwarfs in old days. Inge believed it brought luck in hunting and Julia thought it gave success in love.

The Earl now returned from the woods, and there was still some snow on the sleeve of his black frock. He held out his hands before him, that all who stood in the doorway might make way. His men came in with him and stuck their torches into sockets round the walls and in the corners of the tables, so that the whole hall was bright.

"Friend and Earl," Inge began, "you have a gloomy and

troubled look. You will be of good cheer again when you have heard a Mass."

"I have had a sore task this evening," he answered coldly, and all the young acolytes, who attended at the altar with censers and candles, at once flocked about him and listened in admiration. "That which I had to perform in the forest is accomplished. Now let the men of your escort who were sent on other errands report their doings."

The King's men, who like him wore silver byrnies and blue tunics, began to stir along the benches and one of them arose.

"Not much have I seen to-day," he said. "I have only one thing to report. In the forest I came upon a Finn woman lying prostrate and stiff over a bowl of water with a ripped-up snake in it. She wore catskin gloves like the sibyls. The people said she was called Jorgrimme's daughter and that she had tried to use sorcery against you, King Inge. But it seems the sorcery had turned against herself and killed her. I looked at her awhile and called to mind the saying: The horse that Inge rides cannot stumble."

"It would have been better if she had lived and been brought here to foretell our victory!" cried Julia, letting go the King's fingers.

The whole body-guard joined in a shout of approval, waving to Julia with their gauntlets. A young deacon rose from the farthest bench.

"The King's men are on your side, Julia," he said. "But then you share every day in their games and exercises, and when danger threatens, you are among them, spear in hand. It is not easy to make oneself heard when you have just spoken."

"Do you mean to give me one of the Earl's usual sermons about my sins?" she asked with icy calmness.

"Perhaps I ought to do so, for if you were not against the Earl we should long ago have destroyed Upsala temple and sacred grove with fire. We clerics know full well that in secret you are more devoted to the old religion than the Queen who sits at home in Skara."

Inge frowned. "Were you commanded to tell over the Earl's friends and enemies?" he said.

The young priest trembled and bowed his head.

"Lord, it was not to dispute with your woman that I rose, but to obey our beloved Earl and relate what has happened.

red dye which the Greeks smear on their horses' hoofs to make
them fair to the eye. And if need be we will lay down our
lives for you, Inge!"

"It is of no concern to me whether you will take them into
your service, Inge," said the Earl. "But the Body-guard is already far in excess of its numbers. And you have fifteen
torchbearers and twenty men to wait upon your table and
your bedchamber. It is hard to find lodging for so many."

"All wish to follow me, that is the secret," answered Inge.
"And I will have followers in excess."

At that moment the cock crowed midnight. The tables were
hastily cleared and the horns taken away, while the chaplains
brought in an altar and set all the torches about it. Censers
were swung and the prayers and singing began. Julia still
sat in the high seat playing with her brooches, but Inge knelt
before the altar, tall and broad in the back.

Ulfva had stolen forward between the sons of Folke.

"It is not so much himself that I fear," she whispered. "It
is his many lights and the gentle singing that make me weak
at heart. And still I know nothing of what they have done to
my father!"

Inge noticed her and called: "Ulfva, my sister, come hither
and learn to pray with us, for assuredly you are one of those
who are called."

On seeing that in spite of his words she slipped away into
the darkness, he shook his head with a smile and resumed his
singing. But the sons of Folke had been able to look at her
a moment, as she stood beside them in the light.

"She is somewhat like Holmdis, though she has not the same
hard eyes," said Hallsten. "You may know the Ulfungs by
the straight back. When I heard her childish answers in the
dark she seemed to me quite young. Only when she came into
the light did I see that she was so no longer. It is clear that she
has been living here with her father cut off from all the world.
Be it as it may, she is Holmdis' sister, and therefore she can
rely on us. Go you and speak to her, Ingemund; I am too sad,
it has cost me too much to throw off all my sorrows."

When the last hymn was sung Inge put on a helmet with
hawk's wings and seated himself in a chair before the altar.
Around him stood the whole Body-guard. They were mainly
young warriors, with more thought of falling with honour

than of life, and well used to the summer breeze of success.

"We are still heated and dazed with mead," he said, "but I ask you: Are you agreed that the two strangers be admitted to your brotherhood, simply because they are unafraid and have faith in our fortunes?"

"When did you ever hear a No, Inge?" answered the Bodyguard.

The sons of Folke then went forward and knelt to him. He gave them each a silver-hilted sword, and each sword had its own name. Then the priests chanted a blessing over the new men, who swore on the cross of their swords to follow the King in life and death.

"If you are driven from power," Ingemund promised, "we shall never eat or sleep our fill until we have raised you on our shields again."

Inge embraced and kissed them and ordered the lights to be put out.

"Who was that sighing so deeply?" he suddenly asked. "No, stop blowing out the lights! I heard someone sighing."

"It is not the fashion to sigh in King Inge's hall," answered a voice from the doorway.

"Is it you, brother-in-law? You are a rare and honoured guest. I have not seen you since I was chosen king, and then your voice came near to losing me both throne and kingdom. You were within your rights then, Sven, and I bear you no grudge. Had not the Earl displayed the heavy ears of corn from West Gothland, where they worship Christ, I scarcely know where I should be sitting now. When came you here?"

"Now, while you were at mass,"

"Was it you who sighed? Why do you stand alone there by the door?"

"I am waiting."

"My envoys met you then at sea and you followed them?"

"My men followed them, and when his men go, a chief has to bring up the rear."

"As yet I have not seen your men."

"I find the two best of them are here before me, though they came on foot and I on horseback. Such haste they had, and the roads are good and hard. There is a dearth of snow on the roads this year. Have you thought of the harvest, Inge?"

flakes of scum with a ladle, and around her stood the other women with torches, singing a sombre hymn to the holy mead, the drink of life, which bubbled with secrets and which the gods themselves had brought from the underworld. Each time she bent over the dark surface, which mirrored her form, she uttered an incantation. She pushed aside the bags of spice which swum before her ladle, but their perfume was so strong that it made her think of a warm midsummer day, and she grew quite dizzy.

The scum was collected in a pail for the goats, to please the Hammer God, the helper of thralls and herdsmen. The sign of the Hammer was branded on the handle of the pail, and she kissed it before taking hold of it. Now and again she held out a ladleful to the men who were still awake and had seated themselves at the door to look on. But every man who was offered it had to tell a story before he was allowed to refresh himself.

Ingemund was sitting among these lookers-on and was quickly recognized by his brilliant Varangian dress. With shrewd and calculating glances he regarded Ulfva, who seemed to him a fair and handsome woman, though past her first youth. But he knew that Holmdis, had she lived, would have been older still. When it came to his turn and he had just taken hold of the ladle with all his ten fingers so as not to spill the drink, it was suddenly snatched by other hands. Faces pale and ghastly like the spirits of pestilence appeared in the doorway and eagerly drank instead of him.

"You will thank us later, but now we must brace ourselves," they muttered, and he let them have their will.

When they had rushed out again he said:

"These young priests must be plotting something, as they steal about instead of going to sleep. I noticed in the hall how threateningly they glared at the high seat. It has not escaped me either that the yard dog has been shut up. And there are noises in the stable as of one hafting an ax."

"Who would dare a felon's deed in the house where Inge sleeps?" asked Ulfva, looking up. "You have only hit upon this to take off our thoughts and escape telling a story. You know none!"

"What you say may be half true, Ulfva. I am no wandering skald."

"Then you may drink before you begin, so your tongue will be loosened."

She offered him the mead again. It seemed to him that the honey in the fermented liquor was still humming and buzzing like the bees in the forest. When he had drunk half he said:

"I know but one story; but spare me the telling of it yet."

"Why, do you not know that you will be a laughing-stock if after so noble a gift you try to shirk a good old custom?"

"There is this flaw in my story, that I do not know how it ends."

"We will help you to find an ending if you will let us have the beginning."

"Then let all listen attentively," he said, and emptied the rest of the ladle. "When I have done you shall tell me which of my two heroes is most to a woman's liking. A long while ago there were two brothers, so envious of each other and yet such good friends that whatever the one desired, the other immediately longed for. If they lost a woman, to whom they had both felt themselves bound, it was not long before they began with the same accord to speak of another. They therefore agreed that each should provide himself beforehand with what was necessary for a brotherly rivalry in a bridal bargain. One of them was a wild dare-devil. He clambered up a steep cliff and brought down the rusty iron rings that Olaf Tryggvason had hung there on one of his voyages. The other, who was a wiser and graver man, considered that, as years went by, many pots and kettles would be needed on the hearth of a great house. Therefore he carefully hoarded all the gold he could come by and melted it down into two heavy rings. Answer me now, Ulfva—which of the two men would you have chosen, if they had come to you?"

Her head was so confused that at first she did not understand him. He had to tell the whole story over again, and then the other women began to exclaim. Some declared plainly that they would have taken him who had the incomparable iron rings, others that they would have married him who was provident enough to bring gold to his betrothal.

"And Ulf Ulfsson?" asked Ingemund. "Which of the two would he have chosen?"

"I believe," answered Ulfva, hesitating a moment, "that the

iron rings would have been more to my liking, but that he would have said: You must also pay some heed to his face and eyes, daughter."

The women began to wave the torches with noisy laughter.

"Ulfva, Ulfva!" they cried. "You take after your father. Have you paid so much heed to faces and eyes this evening that you missed seeing the rings hanging at their belts? Our eyes are sharper. We saw with curiosity and wonder that there were both iron and gold rings in the hall."

She looked in innocent inquiry from one to the other, still red-eyed from all the weeping that had choked her. She was the only one who had no heart for merriment, and Ingemund rose and gave her back the ladle.

"A good night to you, Ulfva," he said with bitter harshness. "I have now told you the only story I have learnt, and I must think about the ending as I lie in the straw. It is time I took the men with me. I would it were morning and that I saw Inge ride out to hunt with his bread and berries in his saddle-bag."

When the women were left alone they continued to sing and skim the mead. They had much to talk about and tease one another with, and their shouts and laughter were heard far into the night. But at last they put out the torches and, still jesting, made their way up to the loft which extended over the whole brewhouse. They slammed the door behind them with a loud noise which made many a man wake up and turn over. Time after time they dropped the bar before they got it into place and found the clamp for it. The imprisoned dog set up a howl of complaint from one of the farthest sheds. Then all was silent, and the hour was very late.

Inge was a heavy sleeper and Julitta lay on the bench close by, but Julia sat upright in the bed beside him, looking at the keen, clear stars. Sven's words would not let her sleep. She knew he had the name of being false and was reckoned a bad prophet, but for once his foreboding might chance to be right. At last she felt ashamed of doubting Inge's luck and was about to lay her head back on the pillow, when she saw someone come to the doorway and beckon her.

She dared not ask what he wanted, for Inge was strict about his night's rest and she feared to wake him. So she wrapped his pale-blue cloak about her and walked barefoot to the door.

She recognized the young deacon who had spoken so rudely to her during the carousal. He laid his finger on his lips and pointed to the bed. She nodded approval of his thoughtfulness and followed him rather doubtfully into the darkness. Then she saw a whole ring of young priests and acolytes standing there, and she would have gone no farther.

"We must speak our mind to you sooner or later, Julia," whispered the deacon; "but if you dare not come aside with us, Inge will waken."

"Dare!" she answered with a cast of the neck and walked on a little way. "In the house where Inge sleeps no one need fear. Only I ought to have thought of arming myself."

"We heard Sven's dark warnings, and this time he is a true prophet, Julia. The udalmen fear bad times, and there will be need of the most resolute and diligent man in the land. That is the Earl. It is of this we have to speak with you."

She became more attentive, but at the same time more defiant, and began to listen with bated breath. They had almost reached the stable-door, which stood open. A lighted torch was set in the door-post.

The young priest bent down to her and said:

"Men were too weak to serve God, and so they took to themselves kings to oppose Him. They created them of their own flesh and their own sins, but they made them proud and free withal, so that their subjects could not serve them without humbling themselves daily. They taught their kings to turn men's weakness to account and to make a league with their worst instincts, and only by this means could the kings rule."

"And this you say to me of Inge!"

"King Inge gives promise of better things, and therefore while there is yet time he must be given a warning which will long be remembered. It is not meet that he should drag about with him a woman of your sort. You have been his sun and his joy, but the Cross shall put out your light. Now be it accomplished—in the name of the Church and for Inge, amen!"

Before she had time to answer, she was thrown down upon the threshold and a swift blow of the ax severed her head, which still frowned in furious rage.

"Now the road is straight and open, and the Earl is the mightiest man both here and in the North!" said the deacon, as he raised the head and kissed it on the eyes. "And now I kiss

Inge's woman. How often have I looked with pangs of love on these fair eyes!"

He carried the head into the stable, where Inge's hunting-saddle hung above his horse's stall.

"This shall be Inge's breakfast this morning when he rests in the woods," he said, dropping the head into the saddle-bag. "See what bright stains the fresh whortleberries make upon the cloth."

XIII

For three years in succession the crops had failed, and as the fourth winter drew on there was again no snow. Lakes and ponds were frozen hard as rocks and would bear both horsemen and wagons. Then Folke Filbyter was seized with restlessness and could no longer sit inactive by the fire.

He took his thrall with him and rode out to continue his never-abandoned quest. As before, he was well received both at the robbers' camp-fires and in the houses of the peasants, and all came forward and showed him their hands.

"You must ride to Frey's festival at Upsala," they said. "There will be a great gathering of people from all parts."

Long stretches of good road had been laid by the udalmen and marked with stones, but many houses were shut up, and in them sacrifices were offered to the old gods of vegetation. Everywhere were silence and desolation, and all animal life seemed to have vanished. He rode on and on towards the dark North, which stood like a black wall of rock beyond the pine forests.

After a very long journey he came at last to a heath. From the farms round about came the shrieks of pigs which the women were slaughtering. Heavy clouds of smoke rose far away and the wind brought a smell of burning.

"This must be the land of the Sveas," he said, "where sibyls and sorcerers fill the sacrificial bowls unceasingly with blood. The Sveas cannot live without sacrifice and faith. Here you will lose your tongue, thrall, if you do not mingle the names of the gods with all you say."

But the thrall was seized with reverence for the holy places and threw himself down on the frozen heather.

"Unhappy are you, master, unhappiest among us all, but doubly unhappy since you cannot share my joy."

A house stood by the roadside and the door was open. A bench, still red from the slaughter of the day before, was ranged against the wall. Black puddings, made of meal and blood, were hanging since Yule from a pole on the roof beside a pig's carcass.

The master of the house was dressing for the Thing with byrnie and shield. He seemed to delight in women, for the whole house was full of female thralls both young and old, and a separate wing had been built on posts for them. They pushed each other aside to get a look at the unknown horseman, who seemed strange to them with his iron hat and his chair-like saddle.

"Who is that big man?" they asked. "The fat hangs about his neck in wrinkled folds and yet he is poorly clad. Is he a West Goth?"

"The West Goths have long noses and narrow hands," answered the master. "And they cannot hear a silver spoon fall to the floor without darting their fingers under the table. Woe to us Sveas, who are now so weak that we take our kings from their country!"

"And you Sveas," said Folke Filbyter, "you cannot hear a hog grunt without running a knife into him. By that we know you. I am riding about in search of a vanished son, and I am from the land of millers and robbers south of the forests. You have never yet looked for a king from there."

"What would become of us if even the East Goths thought themselves good enough to be kings in Svithiod! An East Goth always stops at your door to smell what kind of bread is baking. By that we know him. No, stranger, we are not afraid of you. Welcome, then, and let us keep the peace!"

The man showed most attention to the oldest of all the women, and handed her the comb after he had smoothed out his beard with it. Proud of his fine appearance, she stood behind him and combed his hair, which fell down his back.

"If you are bound for Upsala, horseman, our road is the same," he said, looking out of the door.

The rings of his chain mail tinkled, and he playfully pinched the woman's shrunken chin.

"But where are the children, old lady?" he asked. "On a day like this they always use to hang about the threshold to see what is to be seen."

She moved about slowly over the juniper-twigs with which the floor was thickly strewed, laid aside the washing-basin and hung scissors and comb on the wall. Then she stood on a stool and took down five plucked and frozen hens.

"The children have found something else to think about, but now I hear them coming," she said. "You slept heavily last night and woke late, and we women thought there was time enough for you to be angered with hearing a lie. And I would not miss seeing you again in all your glory, like old times. Here are the hens for your tribute to King Inge. We shall see if he'll be content with it, but tell him it's not your fault if you have no corn for him this year. Bad king brings bad harvest."

A band of scared and wide-eyed children came running in and clung to him as he was tying the hens to his belt.

"Father, father!" they cried all at once; "the sacred grove at Upsala is on fire!"

He thrust them aside to go out to Folke Filbyter.

"Who has put such foolishness into your heads?"

"Thing-men, traders, everybody who goes by tells of it, and if you will go up the hill with us you will see the smoke."

"It's not true, it *cannot* be true. Children, you are never to come to me with such a lie again!"

He left the house in displeasure and began to walk beside Folke Filbyter's horse.

"Let me hold on to your saddle, horseman, we shall go the faster. The way is long and slippery. The children are scared with an empty rumour, it is not worth listening to. What would become of their belief if they found one listened to such things? Neither fire nor ax will bite upon that grove. There stands the holy tree which is green winter and summer and which drinks with its roots from Mimer's spring beneath the earth. You may believe me, stranger, if you have never been here before! In the days when I was a child and ran about barefoot as my own little ones do now, that tree was laden with pale fruit—human corpses which the priestesses had washed and soaked in the spring till they were quite white and you could almost see through them. We called this the sacrifice of thralls in place of the King, and thereby we propitiated the gods, for theirs is the land. And in those days they gave us rich harvests, but now the poorest barley will hardly thrive. Therefore we have summoned Inge to meet us at Frey's sacrifice and answer for himself. Horseman, you are old and your pace is slow. Ride faster, faster! If I hold up my sword I can well run. Can it be that the grove of Upsala is burning? No, horseman! Even the Christians durst not do such a deed. The murmuring of that grove was the breath of our bodies, its flowering was our heart. No place in the North was holier."

As he ran, his leather shield and his fowls dangled against his knees, and when the horse was too slow he gave it a blow on the quarters.

Soon they were out on the frozen heath. From every side came udalmen dressed for the Thing, with hens and geese, hams and carcasses of sheep, but the customary loads of grain were not to be seen. They called to each other, telling what they had seen from their homes during the night, when the flames had shot up behind the grave-mounds of the kings. The largest mounds now showed up like distant mountains across the heath, and beside them the morning sun fell upon the solid mass of the temple. The blocks of stone in its walls were alternately round and long and all of different colours. Some were a shining black, still more were green, but the biggest had a red gleam, as though bespattered with blood that could never dry. The charred and smoking remains of the sacrificial grove could plainly be seen at a great distance under the clear winter sky of the month of Goi.

"My own eyes cannot lie," wailed the franklin, holding faster to the saddle-girth as he ran. "I am forced to believe them. But the King's House is not burnt. You have slept well, King Inge. And we shall lay our tribute at your door, as is the law of the realm; but then you shall come out, King Inge. For three days we franklins have held feast for you, and your Body-guard has done its best to see the bottom of the mead-vat. But to-day it is your turn to pay the score—with your skin if need be. Come out to the Thing-mound, King Inge, before the sacrifice begins. There you shall hear franklins' speech!"

On the Thing-mound the King's chair had already been placed on a carpet, and a wide space around the mound was fenced off with hazel posts and blue cords. The spokesmen of the franklins stood nearest the mound; behind each were two men, behind them three, and so on in an ever-increasing circle. Each hundred carried its banner on a pole, and underneath the banner was a bench from which the criers were to repeat what was said on the mound, so that it might be heard even by those on the extreme outside. The crowd of heads grew ceaselessly. At first only a few score, they were soon to be reckoned in thousands. And around the other mounds men were also standing as close as bushes in a thicket. The standards of Fjedrundaland and Attundaland were raised. The men of Tiundaland came marching over the sandy ridge with their Lawman at their head.[17] When all had laid their tribute at the door of the King's House, they advanced into the assembly like a wedge and their speakers ascended the mound and stood above all the rest.

A special enclosure had been railed off for strangers and envoys from the more distant parts of the country, and there Folke Filbyter dismounted from his horse. His thrall had to help him, for he was tired and bent, and like many others of the older men he sat down on the ground.

The thrall led the horse to the long boom to which the riders tethered their mounts. The trading-booths along the road to the Thing were still shut and the sports-grounds were empty. Nor were any women or children to be seen, and although so many men were assembled the chanting of the heathen priests could be heard continually from the temple.

While the men of Tiundaland were still forming up, Inge's Earl ascended to the King's chair, surrounded by his attendants.

He still wore the same simple frock as at Ulf Ulfsson's hall and the wind made his reddish hair flutter around his cap, but his look was bold and undaunted. Weary of the feasting and martial games of the Royal Progress, he was once more face to face with danger and full of energy. Work, work day and night, was his life and delight and his only desire, and it set its mark on the least of his movements. Beside him on the seat he had a chest full of parchment rolls and tables of runes, and he was entirely occupied in examining them. He straightened out the parchments, ran his eye over them and marked the margin here and there with his nail, so as to find the passages he wanted in a moment. It evidently made no difference to him whether he had onlookers or not, whether five thousand people stood around him or only five. His bearing

---

[17] Fjedrundaland, Attundaland, Tiundaland: these three "folk-lands," as they were called, were divisions of the great district of Upland, the home of the Sveas or Swedes proper.

was neither arrogant nor embarrassed, and being entirely absorbed in his official affairs he seemed quite unaware of the threatening silence of the people.

Roused to prayer at midnight and dawn by the crowing of the cock, King Inge had afterwards fallen into a deep sleep. Time after time his body-servant had knocked on the foot of his bed. At last Julitta brought his Thing robes and laid them on the bed-clothes. Then she bent over him smiling, took him by the hair and shook his head.

"Inge, Inge, wake up!" she said, seeing that his heavy eyelids still remained shut.

"Is it prayer-time again already?" asked the King.

"No, you are at Upsala, Inge, and no Masses are sung there; but the people are assembled and wait for you."

"I was dreaming of your sister," he said to Julitta, who was still no more to him than a devoted friend. "It is not easy to forget her."

"Last night when you had gone to bed the younger priests and many of your other men drank her funeral ale. They called it so. At last in their frenzy they plucked the torches from the wall and rushed out into the sacrificial grove. There they set fire to the weird and lofty ancient trees, which for the most part were still full of the skeletons of beasts."

"And the Earl?"

"He lay in his bed, but he did not punish them. He looks pinched and thin, your Earl, but I doubt he is of the kind of starveling that will turn to fat when at last he grows powerful and has his will."

"A stronger and more upright will has never served me."

"I see it is only in your sleep that you remember my sister."

"Yes, it is mostly in my sleep," he answered, suddenly wide awake.

He dressed hurriedly. The servants withdrew the pane of parchment from the window and the cold morning sunshine danced in over the newly lighted fire. His teeth chattered as he stood on the bearskin and his servants placed the golden circlet on his forehead. It was padded inside with blue silk which matched his cloak.

"I repeated to you all last night the words I mean to speak to the franklins and they will be hard words. To-day I shall show them that they have set a lion over them."

He breathed into his broad-fingered gloves to warm them before putting them on, and then he walked briskly to the door.

The horns were beginning to sound about the King's House, and Inge came riding out on a white horse among all the piles of tributary gifts. He carried his sword drawn and the long, sharp blade flashed like a streak of fire. Behind him came all his Body-guard, feudatory barons, chaplains, grooms and guests, a procession which reached from the King's House to the great mounds. But he started on seeing so many more franklins assembled than had ever before attended Frey's sacrifice. In battle, when faced by Magnus Barefoot's Norwegian bowmen, he had never known fear; but the stiff, malignant eyes of these franklins forced him to look down at his horse's hoofs, as though to guide it over the stones with which the road was paved.

"Can Inge's horse stumble?" asked a malicious voice.

Inge felt that it was a bad beginning and tried to rehearse in his memory the proud words he meant to utter from the mound. Some five or six times the evening before, he had announced to his Body-guard what he would say, but now he could recall nothing beyond a promise that his speech should be long and its tone one of command. Almost without knowing it, he gave his horse a dig of the spurs and rode wildly up the mound.

But the customary roar of applause was altogether wanting. He dismounted and received the homage of the Earl, who kissed his hand, while Sven, his brother-in-law, filled the horn for him. But as he was about to drink to the people, the sweet mead sickened him so that he could scarcely take two gulps. White as a sheet he sat in the chair. He saw that it was as useless for him to adopt masterful language as for a shipwrecked man to threaten the storm. True, he was King, but before him stood the King's master—a people in arms.

When the Lawman of Tiundaland had rehearsed the Upsala Law, the Earl opened the proceedings in a dry voice and most of the franklins sat on the ground to rest. Hardly had they laid down their arms, however, when they sprang up again, for the Lawman had ascended to the top of the mound.

At first the Earl feigned not to see him, but the Lawman interrupted his reading and said in a loud voice:

"We franklins have not come this long way to hear your

learning, Earl, nor to vote upon any trifling decrees. Nor do we ask whether it was the Christian who burned our grove, for what is done in the darkness of night partakes of that darkness and remains dark even in the light of day. Nor do we ask whether it be true that you would forbid us franklins to buy and sell freely at our homes in order that the craftsmen and foreign chapmen of Aros and Sigtuna may make the more profit and wear yet warmer furs. We know that you wish to forbid us to hold Thing and to carry arms, and that you would force us to call the Body-guard lords and to pay tithes to the bishops and the Pope in distant Rome. Hitherto it was we who laid foreign lands under tribute and filled our homes with their treasures. We were a free people of husbandmen and had plenty of cattle and good horses. You lay upon us a foreign yoke, and it is none the less heavy for being graced with many ornaments. A man must be as young as you to dream of so many new things. We have not chosen you. You are a fine white loaf from the King's House. The people bake a coarser bread with bran in it. Who was your father and who was your mother? A parcel of priests you call your parents, because they taught you to read. Many rumours are whispered about you, but it was not for your sake we came here. Open your rolls and read the law of kings. The Sveas have the right to make a king or break a king. We ask you, King Inge, will you lay down the power and the kingdom, or will you now come down among us and sacrifice to the old gods for a good harvest?"

The criers repeated slowly and distinctly every word from the mound, and many of the old men had horns with them which they put in their ears to listen.

Sven stood behind Inge's chair, following the shapes of the clouds in the sky. He had not even taken the trouble to change his bleached viking clothes for a Thing dress.

"Last night in the King's House," said Inge, turning to him, "I could speak so clearly about it all. You heard me yourself. Now my thoughts stand still. Yet I am no coward."

Sven regarded him stiffly. "King and brother-in-law," he answered, "the people ask you if you are a Christian. I am not."

Then Inge's tongue was loosened and he sprang up. Pale

as death, but with royal bearing, he stood before the chair.

"Jesus Christ, I am Thine till death!"

The franklins picked up stones and began to throw them at him. Some had brought with them stones big and little in a fold of their cloak, but to begin with they only threw the small ones. A splinter struck him on the lip and filled his mouth with blood.

Sven stood with his head bent, pressing his beard against his chest. He closed his eyes tightly and said to Inge:

"The clouds change their shape and are never alike. There comes a time to every man in his middle age when men suddenly tire of him. They have seen him too often, praised and obeyed him too often. He is no longer either a rising or a setting sun. Therefore they are weary of him. Brother-in-law, you who have so often sat at dice with me must know that at one moment your luck is out and at another you may throw sixes. Good and bad luck always go together like the light and dark scales on a snake's skin. It is of no use to speak of superstition here: when the wise man sees that his luck is out he leaves the dice awhile and waits. This is what I have had to do for four years; and now it is your turn. The cause of most men's misfortunes is that they have not patience to bide their time, but seek to force fortune when it is against them. Another time, maybe, the Sveas will be as ready to shout for you and your laws as they are to-day to stone you. Go back to the King's House and leave me, who have the luck, to throw the dice while my hour lasts. That is the only way to save us both."

"I thought you were one of my friends, Sven."

"I was, Inge; but you must not ask more than you can get. Every man must live to see the very thing happen which in his youth he believed least likely. His best friend will be the one who fails him most surely."

"You are a crafty man."

"Maybe I deserve that character."

"And towards me you have been full of deceit."

"Never in actions, only in my heart."

Inge held his ground proudly and tried to crush him with his look, but within him rose a fear which he could no longer master. The slow and steady shower of stones, getting bigger and bigger, seemed to him more threatening than arrows or spear-points. And yet it was not his fear but his shame of it which at last threw him into confusion.

Surrounded by the shields of his Body-guard, he ran down the mound. The stones fell dully on the leather shields, and with his face streaming with blood he was dragged and carried by his flying attendants into the King's House.

"King of Ruin!" the crowd shouted after him. "King of Bark! King of Famine!"

When the tumult had begun to subside and the doors of the King's House were barred from inside, Sven stepped forward and addressed the Lawman of Tiundaland.

"If I have played falsely with Inge," he said, "it is because I could never be false to the old gods. He and his West Goths are far-sighted and happy, and Christ comes to their rich cornfields with the south wind. It is otherwise with us, stern men of the North, who delight in our priestesses' dark songs of the stars. Glorious was our life in former days, when we lay at sea in our ships. I myself am not much more than a wild berserk, but now I have the nearest claim to your throne. Choose me, and I shall sit in it, even without hope of the future. Last night was a bad night, when many had waking dreams. Last night no good man was to be seen, for they that were good slept. Last night the sacred grove burned, and when the blaze awoke me, I too dreamed a waking dream. I saw the Valkyries ride over Fyrisvall with outstretched hands and clawing fingers. Their ravens swept my helmet with their wings and shrieked like the darkness in the caves under Nifelheim. Their horses were damp and shone like the corpse-covered shores of Amsvartner mere.[18] Their own fair faces were pale and thoughtful. Whom do you seek? I asked. And they answered: A king. We seek a king to bring him to the empty place on the kings' bench in Freya's hall. Can you be he? When we have found him, the doors of the hall will close for ever."

The people rushed up the mound and raised him on their shields and cried in gloomy voices:

"Hail, King after our heart! Hail, Blot Sven and his race!"

[18] Nifelheim (fog-world) is the abode of the dead. Amsvartnir (tawny) is the name of the mere on an island of which Loki lies bound in chains till Ragnarok.

Meanwhile an old man stood in the strangers' enclosure, his face shaded and almost concealed under his great iron hat. Not much did he understand of the new King's speech. He scarcely saw him receive the stone knife, while the sacrificing priests led forward Inge's white horse and held down their bowls to collect the blood. He did not hear the animal's death rattle, for he had his eyes fixed on the Earl. It was the Master of Folketuna.

He was looking less at the Earl's hard and motionless face than at his hands, which were still busy with the rolls, arranging them with almost punctilious accuracy. In the general confusion the old man elbowed his way through the crowd until he finally reached the top of the mound. There he seized the Earl's left hand and held it up to his eyes, but they were running with water and he could see nothing.

"Have I gone blind?" he stammered.

The Earl, who felt he was at the mercy of the people, made no resistance but stared at the round-shouldered peasant in his poor homespun. At last he came to his senses and grasped the grey figure by the chest.

"What do you want with me?" he asked. "When Inge regains his power I shall have your life."

"What do I want with you?" repeated the Master of Folketuna, and his own voice seemed to him so weak that no one could hear it. "What do I want? Ah, you may ask that. Perhaps I have something to say which will mean more to you than all you have heard to-day and make you mild and gentle. And yet I have no more to say to you than to all the others. . . . What shall I answer you? Meet me in secret in the hayloft of the King's House, where strangers are wont to sleep. Come for your own good, even if I find nothing to say to you. You need not hurry. I have learnt patience. Like Sven, I have learnt to wait. Only come, come now at last!"

Those standing by wanted to catch hold of the Earl, but Folke Filbyter was then seized with a solicitous desire to get him down from the mound in all haste. He threw his broad but now somewhat feeble arms around him as a protection, but with a show of violence. And he cried aloud:

"Get you hence, Earl! Go to your deposed master. You have no longer a right to be here."

The stratagem succeeded; the others let the Earl go and

contented themselves with upsetting his chest and trampling on his rolls. Again the Earl thrust his helper from him with an arrogant gesture and went to the King's House.

For a while Folke Filbyter was drawn along with the cheering crowd that carried Blot Sven on their shields. Three times the procession went around the mound and finally into the temple. Through the door Folke Filbyter saw the images of the gods sitting on their pedestals along the wall, perfectly black in the face from the blood with which they were besmeared yearly. Their stiff robes of cloth were hung with precious gifts from chiefs of old time. Though his mind was full of the Earl, he listened to the sagas of the gods and kings told by the franklins around him and tried to catch a glimpse of the weird magnificence within. In the gloved wooden hand of Odin leaned a rusty spear, and the men said: "That is the spear which Erik the Victorious gave to the moody god of Death the same day that he vowed himself to him."—Thor had red human hair and a gleaming gold chain round his neck. All the harpers kissed it and said: "This is one of the chains that Thorvald Hjalte the skald received after the battle of Fyrisvall in reward for his mighty lay." [19]—The people thought too that the sheaf of corn that hung over Frey's seat was made of all the gold and copper that in former years had been thrown into a hole in a grave-mound to buy good years. Frey himself was out, being carried around the fields, but before his empty place stood a round table, on which a bristly golden boar went continually in a ring, nodding its head from side to side and opening its mouth. Husbandmen and smiths sprinkled it with blood and said: "This is Gullinborsti himself, which Sindre made so cunningly from the skin of a wild boar." [20] Everything of iron in the temple was forged from the weapons of vanquished enemies, but iron was the rarest of the metals there. Even the walls gleamed everywhere with plates of gold behind the torches, but the roof was so thickly covered with soot that it was like a starless winter night.

Blot Sven tucked up his sleeves and took small pieces of the

[19] Thorvald Hjalte, an Icelander, though not known to be a skald, sang two verses at the battle of Fyrisvall, for which he was rewarded by King Erik the Victorious.

[20] Gullinborsti (golden bristles) is the boar on which Frey rides. Sindre was the name of a dwarf renowned as a smith.

flesh of the slaughtered horse and went round feeding the gods. Their mouths were round and open, and as the bits of flesh disappeared, a squeaking and scurrying of mice was heard inside the hollow figures. Then he plunged his arms to the elbow in the horse's blood and held them up with outspread fingers before the faces of Thor and Odin.

The harps began to play and the priests danced with flowing locks. The hair of the eldest was singed off; he had fought the flames in the sacred grove to save a last branch of the holy tree, the green leaves of which were long seen shining in the midst of the fire. He handed it with dark incantations to Blot Sven, who placed himself in the middle of the temple by the hanging kettle and stirred the blood and meal with the branch. In another kettle the flesh was boiling. Meanwhile the foremost thanes seated themselves at the tables in order of age and began to drink the broth and eat the fat and liver.

Soon the temple could hold no more people and those who were still outside had to stay beyond the threshold. Folke Filbyter was carried farther and farther away by the crowd until at last he found himself free to direct his steps. Without either hurry or hesitation he left the others and went to the King's stables.

The horses of the Body-guard stood there quite calmly eating from their mangers. Accustomed to rustic ways, he climbed the ladder to the loft fairly easily, in spite of his years. The loft was empty, but a whole mountain of hay lay beside the open hatch in the gable, and there he sat down, for the sun came in.

His misfortunes in recent years had greatly changed him. His face still had the broad fullness of the countryman, but its more sensitive lines had become sharper and nobler, and his red and wrinkled eyelids seemed worn with weeping. He dozed in the sunshine and his bushy hair spread over his shoulders and back. The kettle hat lay on his knee, and with the hay heaped all about him he looked like a buried warrior who had left his mound to thaw his limbs in the fine winter weather.

He wondered whether so great a lord as the Earl would actually clamber up a stable ladder on this day of consternation to talk to an unknown man. It seemed to him unlikely; and yet he believed it firmly and was not uneasy at his delay.

It mattered little how long the Earl waited, if only he did not appear at that instant in all his glory in the dusty loft.

"When I saw him my eyes seemed full of water," he said, "but yet my sight was not so dim as I thought. For I saw something. Or did I only imagine it? Why am I not glad?"

Firm and heavy footsteps sounded below in the stables, and the redoubtable old man began to tremble in all his limbs. But it was only thralls from the temple who had come to choose another victim among the horses. At that moment a harsh voice cried:

"Where are you, man?"

He was powerless to answer, and when he looked up, the Earl was already in the trap-door.

"Is it fear that deprives you of speech?" asked the Earl, coming up to him at once.

"I have forgotten how it feels to be calm," he said slowly. "Do you know what it is to lie awake and think in the midst of your sleep? Do you know what it is to ride from house to house and ask and never find an answer? I have suffered so much that now joy forsakes me, even when at last it should rightly come."

"I understand not a word, old man, save that you desire to beg my favour with some confession or other."

"Your favour is of little worth, methinks, since you and your master are fallen."

The Earl made a gesture of impatience. Folke Filbyter was looking fixedly at his hand, but the Earl continued in the same strain.

"I should not have troubled to come hither, and that so hastily, if it were not my duty to my lord on so perilous a day to pay heed to the smallest thing. Your behaviour was strange and mysterious and led me to suppose that you possess some secret which you think to sell. Granted that for the moment I have lost my power over you, but I will hear you nevertheless. Is it a question of some conspiracy against my life or the King's? How much do you ask for a free confession?"

"What I ask for my confession? Ah, it is not to be measured or weighed! Now I see, now I am no longer blind. Now I can read in your hand. . . ."

The wrinkled face brightened and he raised his trembling

arms, to the Earl, but they sank back on to the kettle hat on his knees.

"You are proud and strong, but I believe you need me and will be grateful to me. No man is powerful enough to stand utterly alone. What do I ask? Nothing that you will not give of yourself. You stand now on a quagmire. Did you hear how the franklins scorned you as a base-born man without father or ancestral home? But I read your past in your own hand. What do I ask? . . . And you wish to know it?"

"Then you read of labour and renunciation. Now I begin to understand. You pretend to be a soothsayer in order to earn a trifle from a rich man. But you cannot deceive me. Your clothes smell of milk, and yet you are no true franklin. Such a one has women to patch his clothes and comb his hair. You are dirty and ragged and unkempt. I noticed you when I stood waiting for Inge. The people laughed at you and were ashamed to see you at the Thing. You are more likely a herdsman who has happened upon an old iron hat and in your simplicity you think it is big enough to hide you."

"What I ask? Can you not feel it within your breast, Folke? I never thought to ask your name. They all call you simply the Earl and fall straight to cursing you. Are you not called Folke?"

The Earl answered with a shrug of the shoulders and turned aside.

"I saw the star-shaped birth-mark in your hand, Folke," pursued the old man. "By that I recognized you. How many times have I kissed that hand when it was no bigger than my little finger!"

"That is enough!" interrupted the Earl. "Have you any secret for sale, or what would you? I remember little of my childhood. Two old priests gave me the birch-rod, that is all I know."

"Then I remember more than you. I am your dead father's father, Earl Folke."

"I call that a bold thing to say. A wild outlaw, lying in the hay in a loft, raises his arms and says, I am father to the King's chief thane! By the holy Virgin, you might act more prudently if you care for your skin!"

"You will find that my boldness goes yet further. A deposed

King has a deposed Earl, and now you need the help of the old outlaw in the hayloft."

The Earl's face flushed deeply.

"Do you seriously ask me to put faith in your crazy fancies?"

"You were always like my own child, Folke, since I had no other. Your father died and my other sons both left me and went a-viking. We will go out to the franklins, my son. They know Folke Filbyter well enough when they are reminded of him. They know the old robber and manslayer. They took him in when he came wandering upon the road with his footsore thrall behind him. They sat by the fire with him and heard him sigh and lament his sorrow."

The Earl walked hastily up and down the empty loft, the planks of which groaned and creaked. Then he stopped suddenly, and so great was his agitation that he was hardly to be recognized.

"This is what I have always feared and expected!" he said in a hoarse and weary whisper. "That one day some adventurer would appear and lay claim to me as you do, because I know nothing of my origin. No, no, my good man, whatever you do, say nothing of this to the franklins."

"Shall I not teach them to stop their insults? Shall I not tell them that you have a father and that he is the Master of Folketuna? What do you mean? Or do you still disbelieve what I tell you? Is there no clue that can help you? Have you not even heard of the Christian preacher who stole you?"

"The preacher?"

"Aye, one of the brethren at Skara."

"And you saw him?"

"His name was Jakob."

"Jakob? It seems as if there was some spark of truth in your presumptuous assertions, man."

"At last I got him in my power, but he was bound by a vow of silence. However much I tortured him, he would reveal nothing, and so I let him starve to death chained to the wall."

"For the sake of human greatness! Now I remember the written words which were told me that dismal evening in Ulfsson's house. So it was my first benefactor who lay dead in his fetters for the sake of human greatness!"

The Earl turned aside, and for a moment his stern features relaxed. The old man felt more sure of his ground.

"Do you see now that I spoke the truth?"

"Don't talk so loud! And remember, not a word of this to others, if you will deserve my favour."

Folke Filbyter bent his head and plucked at the hay about him with shaking hands, collecting it into wisps and scattering it again.

"You are afraid for my life, Folke, your father's life. You are afraid lest the franklins' wrath with you turn also to my destruction, the more so if they begin to think of my past. For though I have house and lands I have always passed for a sort of robber. Yet I should have more to fear from your own Christian King. But now he is caught like an eel in an eel-buck. He dare not even send out his men for a ham or a goose. And when they knocked at the door it was not opened, and that is why you were so quick to come and seek me in the stables. Perhaps when it is dark he will venture on flight, not before, and then if you cannot slip out with him you will be left like an ownerless horse. Then it may be a good thing for you to go home with me and stay under my lowly roof till the storm is over."

"It will be a brief squall with sunshine to follow. Listen to the bellowing of the victims outside and judge for yourself whether that can help us now. Blot Sven is a dreamy viking who loves to sit at mead and listen to the sound of harps, and there the lightning shall strike him. I am not one to be an ownerless horse, my friend. To me it is painful not to have work to do, and I shall not rest till I have helped Inge back to power—nor then either. How much do you ask to hold your tongue about this tiresome story?"

"Just now you asked me what I would have to reveal it. And that you could not see without asking! The son did not know what the father in such case asked in return. I asked for the only thing left for a crushed heart to long for. And now you would already have me hold my peace about it; nay, perhaps you would rather I took back what I have said."

"You spoke of a Christian preacher," said the Earl, trying to put on a stern look, but his eyes were shifty and abashed. "I remember an old man of pure life who sometimes came to see me when I was a child among the priests of Skara. His

name was Jakob, and I remember him with love. He was a
kindly man and he exhorted me never to search for my father
but to believe and work."

"Then why did he not stay with you?"

"He preached heresy, and at last the priests forbade him
altogether to instruct me. After that he disappeared from my
life, silently and hastily, as I had always seen him move. I
grew up, and Inge became King. He wanted an Earl who was
fit for more than wearing the fine clothes of a thane. The
priests recommended me—and at one step I stood next to the
King. To bear such fortune without a fall, a man needs
wisdom."

"And Jakob never uttered the name of Folke Filbyter?"

"Never . . . that I remember. But I think I have heard
the name before, though it was much later. It was in Ulf
Ulfsson's country, and later here at Upsala. Two brave men,
who had been in Micklegarth with the Varangians and there
been baptized, were afterwards taken into Inge's service.
Their names were Ingemund and Hallsten. To-day they are
in charge of Inge's wagons and tents yonder on the sandy
ridge, and therefore were not at the Thing. Good franklins'
blood is still reckoned as high birth in our land, but it has been
whispered that their father was an ill-famed robber of your
name. They do not deny it, though they say in his excuse that
he has house and lands. To him they will not return, since
they have accepted the Christian faith. I remember this now.
I am in no wise ashamed of kinship with such good men, but
I must take counsel with them. Our intercourse has not been
of the best, but if they find that the Earl is their nephew,
they will perhaps let bygones be bygones. Your news has
come upon me so suddenly, whether it be a crafty lie or mixed
with a grain of truth, that I cannot yet think clearly. We must
act prudently, my good man, and I promise to take care of
you for the rest of your days if only you keep silence. For
a King's minister in my position it is a hazardous adventure
suddenly to be given a father."

Folke Filbyter sat for a long time in silence, plucking at
the hay, abashed and shy in the presence of his own grandson.
When at last he answered, his own voice seemed to him to
belong to another, to one he had left far behind.

"So Ingemund and Hallsten are here too! . . . I never

thought I should live to see so much joy at once. You are right. Go and fetch them. I long to see them before I die; but believe me, Folke, it was you I loved best. No man can control his heart, and it was you alone I have sought for all these years."

The Earl was already half through the trap-door.

"Stay where you are and rest in the hay," he said. "I rely upon your silence."

Folke Filbyter nodded to him, but when he was left alone he said to himself—and now he recognized his own voice:

"I am not happy. My heart has only grown heavier. I looked in his hand, and he is the stolen child of Folketuna. Then why have I travelled the roads for a generation, searching and questioning everywhere, if I am not to feel happy now?"

XIV

FOLKE FILBYTER sat dozing and sighing in the sunshine, but now and again he was violently recalled to the present by the noisy crowd outside the temple.

A long table had been set up, reaching almost to the King's House, and the servants of the temple had much to do. These were voluntary thralls who out of zeal had devoted themselves to the gods to serve them at the great festivals, but at other times were free men living at home on their land. The servants of Frey and Odin wore green and blue kirtles, but those who had devoted themselves to Thor were in red, and only those who had red hair and beards might serve him. It was the part of Odin's thralls to stir the blood and meal together and bake the black blood-loaves which were so big that they reached across the table. Thor's thralls set out the rich creamy milk in which the people dipped the broken bread, and Frey's brought round the roasted boars and sucking-pigs on spits. There were also black thralls, but they were pardoned thieves. The franklins spat on them and called them scarecrows, for their only duty was to run about with brooms scaring away ravens and crows. In spite of them the fat, shiny birds made bold to hop on to the very table, since they were sacred and none might hurt them under pain of death.

Slaughtered horses, dogs and hawks were plunged into the sacred spring and then hung up on the charred trees. Farther off men stood in groups around boiling cauldrons or helped each other to hold down oxen and swine while they were slaughtered. But this was only done for the sake of the reeking blood, for the victims proper were killed within the temple, where all preparations were made beforehand. By degrees the whole charred grove was filled with death-cries. On the frozen sward all footprints were swimming in blood, and the table and benches bore marks of bloody fingers.

Seven and twenty carcasses were now hanging in the trees and the carrion birds hurried from the table and the place of slaughter to peck out their eyes. Then all at once a general singing and shouting arose, as though the scent of blood had thrown the crowd of franklins, hitherto so grave and glum, into the wildest frenzy. But it was not only the streams of blood that had had this effect. Nor was it the opening of the trading-booths, nor yet the arrival of fur-clad merchants from Gandvik, offering for sale their beautiful female slaves, who sat two or three behind one another on a horse.[21] A few vikings from the nearest ships collected about the bare-legged riders, but as yet they had no thought of outbidding each other. It was something else, which the assembly had long been expecting and now greeted with a rising storm of applause. Three vats of mead, well wrapped against the cold with cloths and twigs of spruce, were drawn round the temple on sledge-runners and then set up each in its tent, where all who came might help themselves. After them came a sledge drawn by women and boys; it had a canopy above it and on the seat stood Frey's image, bereft of its robes and entirely naked. The men rushed forward and hacked and stabbed at the god with their swords. Finally the oldest of the women pulled him down on to the ground and belaboured him with heavy rods, to the ends of which cocks' feathers were attached.

"How do you think crops will grow in the tired and sleepy earth!" they cried as they flogged him more and more madly. "You are old and wintry, Frey, and you must die, that you may rise again in youth and fertility!"

The harps twanged and the newly chosen King appeared at the door of the temple. The noise died away and the women lay down and put their ears to the god, whispering that now he was dead. Then they began to clothe him in precious robes for his resurrection. While this was going on, toasts were drunk; first to Odin for victory and power, then to Thor for freedom and manly courage, and then to Frey for growth and plenty. When the Bragi beaker was brought out,[22] Blot Sven emptied the horn at a single draught and went forward to Frey, who was now lying on a bier, ready to be carried into the temple to rise again. When he had sprinkled the faces, hands and

[21] Gandvik is the White Sea.
[22] Bragi's toast was an indispensable part of the ceremony at all festivals. It was the custom to make solemn vows over these toasts. Bragi was a son of Odin and was connected with the art of poetry.

clothes of the bystanders with blood, he held the sacred branch
over Frey—the last green of the season.

"I hear the roar of the World Mill," he said. "Sleeplessly
the giantesses grind. I hear the march of Time. So long as
my years last, I will support the tottering temple. After that
I await you without regret, pale spearwomen. You have grown
old and wintry, Frey, and you must die, that you may rise
again in youth and fertility. Yet there was a time when the
people were not content to thrust at your image with their
swords, but sacrificed their own kings. And now I turn to you,
Sveas! Of a work half done nothing is to be hoped. If we
waver to-day, Frey's sacrifice will soon be abandoned. There
in the King's House sits Inge, my brother-in-law. If your
hearts are brave, fetch him hither and let the priestesses whet
their knives."

He looked expectantly from one to another, but they were
busy sheathing their swords and the clouds stood white and
motionless in the sky. The merry hubbub that had greeted
the god was swept aside and the momentary excitement fell
like a mask from their gloomy faces. No horns or wooden
cups were filled at the mead-vat, and some threw theirs away.
The meats were left untouched on the table, and grown men
sat down and wept.

Trade, which had hardly begun, ceased altogether at the
booths. The merchants from Gandvik took their horses by the
bridle and led their fair slaves aside. All turned to the King's
House, as though expecting every moment to see Inge rush out
with his Body-guard, carrying the Christian Cross on high.
All felt that the old faith was dead. A terrible foreboding
forced itself upon men and women alike and strangled their
throats so that they could neither lament nor threaten, and
the shadows of the hovering carrion birds passed over their
heads. But still all was silent and calm, the whole King's
House seemed plunged in sleep, holding nothing but silent
vows and oaths of a day of vengeance.

The solitary old man sat huddled up in the hay-loft, but
the very stillness made him start. He closed his withered eyelids again in the strong sunshine.

"You have grown old, Frey," he muttered to himself, half
aloud. "You have grown old and wintry, and you must die,
that you may rise again in youth and fertility. Those words

are for you too, Master of Folketuna. I have ploughed and
gathered in and have reaped enemies and hatred and shame,
and now I see that all is but a beginning. I thought it was for
myself I gathered riches, but it was for others. For their sake
it was that I landed among the skerries and built my Folketuna. So little did I know, so little have I understood. I
thought my life was as soft clay between my hands, when I
myself was the soft will-less clay. I have seen my own offspring, and I see them grow up and multiply, generation after
generation, and it is the length of time that frightens me. Better were it if man lived but a single day, but with the strength
of a young god, and begat his children in the evening and
then vanished. What avails me now the locked chest at home
with all its heaped treasure? I could never see why two
upright pieces of wood, called high-seat posts, should confer
honour on a man, and it seemed to me that my straw was
good enough to sleep in. But now I would have hangings on
my walls and bearskins on my floor and cloths on my tables
and the whole house full of fiddlers and minstrels, that my
sons might be proud of me and say: this is our father! Aye,
now I would have all this, and now it is too late! By craft
and mockery I have been tricked into toiling like a beast of
burden, and I have grown weary under the lash and nobody
thanks me. I see the tree grow and branch out, and I myself
am only the clumsy, ugly seed which was buried in the mould."

He began to sway slowly backwards and forwards and the
sunbeams danced over him.

"I knew well enough that by this time you must be a grown
man, Folke; but in my thoughts you were always a little child
sucking milk out of the bull's horn. I have never really been
able to picture to myself what it would be like to meet you in
the flesh after all these years. I believe it would have been
better if I had found you on the road, poor and hungry, and
lifted you on my horse and ridden home with you and put you
to bed and tended you as of old. Then, after you were rested
and fed, we should have opened the chest with its noisy bolts
and locks. I should have laid out gold chains and silver ingots before you and counted every coin in the bags for the
hundredth time. Then I should have gone and counted the
thralls, calling each one by his nickname. You would have
seen how well fed and warmly clad they all were. We should

have gone into the stables and looked at the horses, and you would have been eager to count the well-kept, silky-coated cattle. At last we should have gone out into the fields, where I should have picked up lumps of earth and crumbled them in my fingers to show you that it is the best and richest soil to be found. Why has it not turned out as I so fervently desired?"

He continued in this fashion, tormenting and consoling himself by turns, now silently, now aloud, although he could already hear voices and the ring of silver spurs in the stable below. There was a noise and a hum as of a flood in springtime.

He recognized his own family by their speech, and was only surprised that three men could make such a clatter. With a feeling of dejection he turned towards the trap-door. The Earl appeared first on the ladder, and behind him came Ingemund and Hallsten in their brilliant accoutrements.

"How white and old he has grown!" Hallsten whispered.

"You may safely speak up," said the Earl. "At his age hearing is feeble. When I was here before and called to him, it was a good while before I had an answer. So you recognize him? You are quite sure?"

"There cannot be the least doubt that he is our father," said Ingemund decidedly.

"Come nearer, my sons! My eyes have grown weak," said Folke Filbyter, though he knew in himself that he both heard and saw correctly. But there was distrust in his soul and he wanted to tempt them to greater frankness.

Yet, as the three stood before him, he thought he had seldom seen finer men. Their features were firm and open. The eager brightness of their bearing showed emulation, a desire of taking part in great contests and always bearing off the prize. All the healthy, unspoilt vigour of their young race, in which the peasant's blood still flowed, was concentrated in a craving for activity which knew neither care nor weariness. This he could read in their faces.

"I thought it was the custom even among King's men to greet one's father," he said, rebuking their hesitation.

Hallsten at once hurried forward, with his silver-embroidered cloak fluttering about him, bent his knee and kissed his father's hands. Ingemund followed him less impulsively.

I. Here y
gate.—The
ashamed of

"For tha
but Folke I

"Come h
thing to co
half."

"Will yo
doubt?"

"No; you
your head
father. Do
ing on it?
I am not n
much more
a-viking, an
other wayfa
to the brim

The Earl
looking at i
voice.

"Has he n

"He fitted
to be busy l
before, whe
There were
gold, but I
a feeling th:
To us you
whether you

"Hallsten
attentive by
gained some
at the Thing
ther. I shu
it will be eas
in your chest
he has a han
trustful of u
but we have

"And you, Folke?" asked the old man, holding out his hand.

The Earl did as the others, and before he had time to rise Folke Filbyter pressed his head to his heart.

"Have I at last got you back, Folke? It was so long, so long to ride about the roads and search. But how is it peace does not return to my heart? Why does the wound bleed afresh, why do I suffer now as I did on the day you were taken from me? A strange fear grows and grows within me. And you have never once called me father?"

The Earl freed himself rather roughly from his embrace and stepped back.

"The franklins might see us, father, and that is not fitting," he said, red in the cheeks from kneeling. "And you always speak too loud, father. At the King's court one must learn to whisper."

"It seemed otherwise when you came in just now. I have no fear of the franklins, children. They do not tear each other to pieces. I have scorned and thrown down their gods, but I have never crawled before the mighty, and such conduct brings a man honour in his old age."

"And what images have you cast down?" asked the Earl.

"Freya's and Christ's Mother's and maybe more. I did not count them."

Ingemund and Hallsten exchanged a glance and crossed themselves several times. The Earl smiled a little and patted the old man on the shoulder.

"Now understand us, father," he said with some embarrassment but an attempt at friendly confidence. "We do not wish to fail in filial respect and we are no vainglorious fools. We are only young and strong and we mean to make our way in the world. There is sound stuff in us, and we have you to thank for it. When was ever a man of my years chosen Earl? But in our position it is better to be of unknown birth than to come from a home that is ill-famed, especially among the baptized. I have taught Inge to be nice about name and birth. The church of Skara was my mother and its priests my fathers. Therefore we beg you have a care that neither the franklins nor the Body-guard hear anything. In disturbed times like these you might easily ruin your own children. We are all three agreed about this. It was my aim to wrest the power from the stubborn franklins and place it in the hands of

Inge's
if the
wear
"De
scarce
King.
only j
"Yc
bygon
go wi
you m
when
see th
your l
that w
"I
You a
milk,
"Th
cially
us yo
the ri
condit
Foll
to get
quietly
about
"I t
would
home.
welcom
my ba
for ho
well a:
one da
race,
childre
Now l
you be
see th
see my

must see how all is changed by what you have just told us. By great gifts to the Church you may obtain forgiveness for many things."

"Perhaps I ought never to have said it. Perhaps I ought to have appeared poor and homeless in order to know you better, for we all need gold and silver ingots. It was not to aid a Christian king and his priests that I followed the plough. The key hangs here inside my shirt, Folke. And now I will tell you another secret. There it shall stay as long as I live."

"Well, well, father, we will think no more of Inge. But when he is king again and we three have firm ground under our feet, we shall ride to your house with a splendid retinue and call you father before the whole people. You do not know how high I stand in Inge's favour and all that he will do for me. He even has plans of marrying me to a woman of the Danish royal house. To such a height will he raise Folke Filbyter's blood, because I have always served him unselfishly."

"And I, Folke, how can I help in this?"

"You can change your rags for more suitable garments and begin a new life. It would be poor gratitude to Inge thoughtlessly to destroy all by exposing oneself to the scorn of the mob. We have need of patience. The evil that is spoken of Folketuna will be forgotten more readily if you make a display of your wealth. In that way it will serve both you and us. Then we shall be able to sit at your feet and no contempt will dare to dog our steps. Our hearts are not so hard as they may seem from our hasty speech. The respect which we shall then be able to show you openly will spread by degrees to others. When the time comes you shall receive us in your rich home with honour and magnificence. But to-day we will not rashly pull out an old man from the hayloft and say: Sveas, here you see the Earl's father!"

Folke Filbyter took a few steps forward and all three respectfully hurried to help him. "Thanks, thanks, my dear children, but I have still some strength left. I am not used to be supported by servants. And thanks for your open speaking, Folke. You, who have become a mighty man while still so young, understand it all much better than I. Let me once more press you to my breast. Ah, I could stand so with you in my arms for hours, forgetting all I have gone through, forgetting all around me. It does not bring me happiness, as

I had expected, but it is like a moment's sleep and rest—an
uneasy rest, but still a rest. Your hair is so soft to the touch,
and when I hold you thus, it seems as though you too were
asleep. I have confessed the truth, Folke; it was you I loved
best. And now I will say farewell to you, my children, and
wish that all you seek for may be yours. I believe that at last
we begin to understand one another. Let me now go home.
. . . Never did I know that a man could sink into such misery!"

He gently pushed them from him, but Folke would not
leave him and followed him to the ladder.

"No, father, you must not leave us with words like these.
There is only one deliverance, and it is that you accept baptism. I too have a key under my frock, but the treasure it
opens is imperishable."

He took out the silver cross and held it over the old man.

"Repent and believe."

"You speak of what is impossible."

"Pray for strength."

"I cannot."

The Earl's eyes flashed fire and red spots appeared on his
cheeks.

"I command you to take baptism, man. It is the Earl who
speaks."

"Why do you torment me, Folke?"

Hallsten took hold of the cross and moved it aside.

"Let him be, Earl. He has lived according to his lights and
he will not yield."

"Hallsten, you have the best heart of the three," whispered
Folke Filbyter. "Though I said just now I did not need your
help, I must ask for it, for my eyes are so dim that I cannot
see the rungs of the ladder. Thanks, thanks, my children.
Just bend a little and hold me under the shoulders. Now I
am down, but it will be better if you stay up there till it is
dark. I hear the people are still noisy."

Without looking back he made his way through the crowd
which was still staring at the King's House. He found the
thrall with his horse, and when he was in the saddle he pressed
the iron hat on his head again and, greeted by one or two
taunting cries, rode away over the heath.

He made no haste but let his horse go as slowly as it liked.

They had heard it was the King's Earl with his nearest kinsmen. They were now visiting the Ulfungs' hall to fetch Ulfva, who was clad in the bridal dress.

Next morning, when the cock began to stir on his beam, Folke Filbyter said:

"I hear that King's men are in the district, but do I look as if I could receive such great folk in fitting state? For that I am too old and tired. It is better that I spare myself the trouble. As an old husbandman I know that the day when the corn is cut is not less joyful than the day of sowing. Once I was superstitious, but how should I be afraid of death? Have I not died times without number in the course of my long life? Have I not died every evening, when I fell asleep and lost myself in dark visions and fancies? There is nothing left me of what I had when young, neither my skin nor my yellow hair nor my senses. What was then my joy is not so now. The man I was then is gone long ago and would face me as a hostile stranger if he came back. To turn and leave the man I am now, gives me but little fear. Therefore I rejoice to see that the hour has come for me to open my veins, as I know the men of my race have done before me. Bring hither all I need, and when the blood has run out and I am still, you are to lay me in the mound."

The thralls were not surprised, for they had asked one another why he persisted in living. Without either hurry or hesitation they took a pewter dish and filled it with water. They set it before him on a stool, which they pushed in between his knees, so that it stood under his chest. Beside the dish they placed a towel and the stone knife which in his younger days had been used in sacrificing.

Some of the women went out to fetch wild flowers and fresh hay; the others helped him to turn down the shirt from his chest, but while they were doing so, one of the thralls cried out:

"You will have no time to cut yourself, master; you must put it off awhile. We can't receive these christened lords with sacrifices. We hear the sound of their horns already among the oaks. Be quick, women, fasten the shirt again and cover up the bowl!"

The women threw the stone knife into the water, covered the bowl and put it out of the way. It was high time, for the King's men rode up at full speed and it was not long before the whole meadow in front of the gate was full of them. The horns were blown and there were so many tassels and bells on all the harness that it seemed as though a swarm of bright insects buzzed around each horse's head.

On a milk-white steed with red trappings and reddened hoofs sat Ulfva in her bridal dress, and behind her was carried a tall wooden cross with the image of Christ. On the pole hung a severed head, and though its features were yellow and distorted, everyone could see that it was the Elk the Club King's. The terrified thralls ran hither and thither and tried to bar the door, but one of the horsemen was at their heels and forced it open. Nearly falling over his silver spurs, he rushed up to the hearth and his locks danced about his beaming face.

"Ho there, you thralls, we are friends and no enemies!" he cried with a gay laugh. "I am Hallsten Folkeson! Is there none among you who recognizes me? And here comes Ingemund, the strong champion in Christ, and here is Folke, the King's Earl. Make way for him, that his clothes may not brush against you. Stand up along the wall with your arms crossed! Thus thralls stand before thanes. But how have you served and tended our father, you whom he clothed and fed? He sits there in rags and almost barefoot! We little knew he was in such a plight. Can you forgive us, father, for being so long in coming?"

Hallsten's blue eyes were filled with tears, and he drew his father's shrivelled hands from under the mangy wolf-skin. Overcoming his repugnance, he kissed them again and again. When the Earl and Ingemund saw this, they bowed down and did the same.

"We could not tell that he wished it otherwise," answered the thralls, ashamed of themselves. "And he has never given up the key of the chests; he wears it next his skin."

"Then now you shall be taught other ways," said the Earl. "Now Blot Sven's followers have perished in the flames and he himself is slain. I come with three hundred horsemen from King Inge's court in West Gothland to root out the last remnants of heathendom in this land. And I shall strike hard. But I have another duty, and one no less near my heart. Inge has sent me with an honourable gift to your master, whom henceforth I openly acknowledge as my father before the world. For my sake Inge will spare him, though he clings to the old faith, and his gift speaks for him. Here you may see it. It is a bull's horn which I had with me as a child; afterwards it stayed with the brethren at Skara. They had heard many heathen legends about it, and on it is written the name Månegarm in runes."

"By that horn we know you again," said the thralls, clinging to the wall in fear and astonishment.

"I place the horn here on the bench beside you, father. Once it had rude feet of iron, but now they are of red gold. This is a symbol of the change in my estate. And at every house we came to we have declared that we were on our way hither to do homage to our father, the rich and powerful master of Folketuna, best known perchance for the wild deeds of his youth, but also praised for his faithful longing for us, his children."

Ingemund then began to speak. He clapped the old man cheerily on the shoulder, making his own sword shake in the scabbard. And it was no longer of wood but of steel and silver with Inge's hawks on the sheath.

"Lift up your head, father, and leave off sighing. The dark years are over. Out there Hallsten's bride is waiting, the daughter of your worst enemy. She is now grown into a fair woman, though we still sometimes call her little, since her sister was so much older than she. It must not surprise you that she will not enter a house where her sister suffered so much. But she sends you the noble assurance that she will forget. And with her knowledge of the country she has helped us in many ways. Her own proud birth you know; but she has admitted that Jorgrimme and his daughter according to legend were descended from mighty Finn kings of old time. This is a thing to be considered now, since Inge seeks a brilliant marriage for the Earl. Your offspring are of high and noble birth, Folke Filbyter."

The Earl nodded approval, but he was sunk in thought. His black frock showed up against the silvery glitter of the others' dress and its coarse, thick stuff, designed for warmth but not for ornament, hung loose about his muscular frame. He thrust his thumbs into his plain leather belt and the harshness sometimes faded from his face, but the seriousness never.

"Was it by this wall he starved to death, my first bene-

factor—for the sake of human greatness? I can still trace
the words he wrote, glorifying injustice and his own fate."

"He was out of his wits at the last," whispered the thralls.

"No, he had his wits better than any of us."

"Maybe we shall be able to write another line about the injustice on the walls of Folketuna," said Hallsten, but the Earl
did not hear him.

"And was it here I was born," he said, "in this bare and
grimy hall? Was it in that corner that my mother lay and
died? I must own that all is not as I had expected. Sometimes I dreamed of a prouder and brighter home. Knowing
nothing, I could imagine so much that was fair. What dreams
a man may have, whom no one dares to undeceive! In the
impenetrable mist he can see all he desires: high-seat posts
hung with shields, and noble, happy women about a cradle.
Often I pictured to myself my mother as the young wife of
a fallen chief, who in her flight had hidden me under a bush
in the forest. I thought I could see how the charitable friar
found me there and baptized me in the spring to a life of toil.
A foundling, cried a voice within my breast, an orphan has
none but Thee for Father, Thou Almighty through the ages!
And Thou shalt teach me to carry Thy banner. Now Thou
hast humbled me, but not bent me, for before me lies a way
of light. And it leads eternally upward!"

He looked around upon the naked walls, where the dust was
so thick among the cobwebs that they looked like hanging bats,
and upon the floor, where the hens continually ran about among
the feet of the thralls. But he closed his eyes to all this and
soon saw nothing but his own bright future, and his words
fell faster and ever prouder.

Hallsten was the only one who stayed by the old man, sitting beside him on the edge of the hearth.

"You must look at our tunics, father," he said. "The
Christian Cross is embroidered on the breast, and from it
flows strength. Not long can we stay with you. Blot Sven
has a son, a heathen like his father. He has hidden himself
in these woods and with him we must do battle. The spoil
will be ours, we are promised all his lands. But for this
we could not have thought of visiting you so soon. The people all think we are come only for your sake and for my wedding, and this thought lulls the heathens in security. You can-

not imagine how light our hearts are when success everywhere attends us. If a stray arrow sings in the air, it never strikes us but always our enemy. If a rotten tree falls, it does not crush us but our pursuer. But why talk of enemies when all run to meet us and promise their help! Fortune is with us and none can resist her. You must rejoice with us, father, sitting at home in the ashes and thinking of your young race. Father, you must be the first to wish luck to the Folkungs!"

"Aye, woe to the man or woman who would stand in our way!" said the Earl. "Father, clothe yourself in scarlet, fetch fiddlers and drummers to your hall, for one day it may fall to you to feast King Inge."

Hallsten combed the hair from the old man's forehead with his fingers and, bending down, looked into his face.

"That day may soon be here, if we succeed, and succeed we shall. None of us has yet been defeated. We shall send you cushions for your bench and hangings for a canopy, if you will give us wherewithal to buy them. It has cost us dear to fit out our horsemen and at present we have nothing left. But now I will give you a piece of advice whereby you may win Inge's favour. Begin in good time to scrape the soot from your roof and to gather nuts, for Inge loves fresh nuts. You can go out yourself to the bushes and pull down the branches with your stick and pluck them, and that will pass the time. And with every nut you drop into your bag, think that each moment is worth a thousand times more to your sons. We are men in a hurry. At your age a whole long winter has no more to offer than a single day, but you must rejoice with us, father. The beams of your hall are low and I feel I am scraping my hawk's wings to pieces, but you must give me a new pair. We have no time now to take off our armour. I hear our men sounding the horn again; that is the signal that we must not stay too long."

Folke Filbyter, who had sat in silence listening to his sons' stream of words, fumbled under the wolfskin on his chest.

"Come here, Folke," he said. "You must help me; my hands are so stiff. Here is the key on my breast; have you found it? You are to go to the middle chest and take out cups and dishes, that my guests may be served according to their noble station. Is there beer in the house, thralls? What is that you say? There has been no beer to drink for ten years?

Why, then it must be so. Set forth milk at least, and bread, and what there is."

The Earl took the key and opened the chest. The lock creaked and grated and the iron bars fell heavily on the ground. Folke Filbyter moved to the side of the hearth nearest the chest and his eyes did not leave his sons. Ingemund and Hallsten helped the Earl to lift the lid. When at last they had raised it, all three were astonished.

"I never thought to see so much treasure," said the Earl, sinking his voice to a whisper, but at that moment Folke Filbyter would have heard a grain of sand fall. "It seems that now we could afford to make the atonement for ancient wrongs which the Ulfssons claimed at the marriage. But they are my mother's brothers and have taken baptism and will be useful allies to us if we are careful to gain their friendship. Let us then rather give them the whole of Folketuna to be their dependent manor; thus it will soon be forgotten with all its dark deeds. It is true that the law forbids the alienation of ancestral estates, but I shall speak to Inge. It will be best for us, and they shall be free to give the place a new name."

Ingemund knelt down to examine the contents of the chest. It was filled with beads of amber, cornelian, rock crystal, gold and silver. He had to push them aside to get at the great vessels at the bottom. There he found nothing less than an image of Christ's Mother in a tabernacle of gold. He answered the Earl in the same low tone:

"I fear that for our own sakes we shall have to dip deeply in the chest when the old man is laid in the mound. After all he was our father, and there is no help for it, Earl, we must build a church to expiate his memory. If you take my advice it shall stand on that knoll that the goatherds in my childhood called Bellerbo or Bellbo. Stones lie there already in plenty. From the silver we can cast a splendid bell which will be heard for miles when it is rung for the repose of his soul. Of the rest we truly have good need ourselves. Listen to me, father!" he cried, raising his voice gaily, as he stirred the contents of the chest. "You are richer than we thought. You must help us to maintain our troop, and soon we shall have to buy fresh horses. Fortune is not to be bribed with empty hands."

"So long as I live, nothing shall be taken from the chest," answered the deep and tremulous voice from the hearth. "No-

He stood and watched them depart. Many of his household were gathered about the door, but after a while the women began to place fresh hay under the benches and strewed it with the fairest wild flowers. Then all the thralls, male and female, went out, except one. He stayed to close the door from within, as was the custom at a house-sacrifice.

The causeway thundered under the hoofs of the Folkungs' troop and soon they reached the nearest stretch of forest. Hallsten's bride sat in the saddle in front of him and he played with the ring on her finger, holding it up before her in the sunshine. When the three kinsmen came out into the open again, they set spurs to their horses and fixed their eyes on the edge of the next wood. There the unknown awaited them, fresh deeds and new lands to be won. All three rode abreast, talking of gain and worldly success.